MURDER IN TOLLAND

A Mystery Novel

David M. Hamlin

Van Rye
PUBLISHING

Cover design by Jason B. Hamlin

Published by Van Rye Publishing, LLC
Ann Arbor, MI
www.vanryepublishing.com

ISBN: 978-1-957906-12-6 (paperback)
ISBN: 978-1-957906-13-3 (ebook)
Library of Congress Control Number: 2023941066

Dedication

For Sydney, the muse who sings to me every day.

Chapter 1

IKE KARAS was dead.

He was stretched out on a chaise lounge on the expansive teak deck that overlooked his sloping backyard, wearing expensive pajamas and a red silk robe with black piping. A coffee mug and a half-eaten blueberry muffin sat on a low table beside the lounge.

Jimmy Dalton found the body. Everybody else used the front door for deliveries, but this Karas guy had made a big deal out of getting his paper on the deck. That demand annoyed Jimmy since it made his route longer. Plus, the guy never tipped on collection day, which was even cruddier.

Jimmy's old man made side money delivering the Hartford Courant to the developments and older outlying houses while driving a filthy but well-maintained pickup truck. To save time and gas, he made Jimmy deliver to the houses on the Tolland Green. In good weather, Jimmy could bike the papers around efficiently; on less pleasant days, he walked the route, sometimes listening to snow scrunch under his boots or making sure his scarf stayed high on his cheeks and nose. In any weather, Jimmy didn't much care for the assignment, but it allowed him to "earn" his allowance.

Once he figured out the man wasn't just dozing in the early morning sun, Jimmy let out a holler and ran next door to get somebody to call a doctor or an ambulance. That was at 6:35.

Before 7, news of the death had reached every house on the Tolland Green except for Zoey Caldwell's cottage; Zoey was in New York for a few days. It took a bit longer for word to reach the homes beyond the Green, including the modern homogenous development houses that some long-term residents called "New Tolland." Still, by noon, all but a few of the town's 15,000 residents knew Karas was dead.

In the heart of summer, Jimmy spent his days swimming and horsing around at Crandell's Pond. On the day he found Karas's body, Jimmy got to the pond ahead of most of the usual group. He figured his direct proximity to a dead body and a cursory interview with the police would give him an extra measure of "cool" with his peers and a large serving of awe among the littler kids. He was right. His social status was so elevated that he counted that day among the best of that summer.

At about the same time Jimmy Dalton dove into the cold pond water for the first time, when the sun had fully risen and made towel-drying quick, Demetrius Clarke pulled into the dirt parking lot beside the Tolland Inn. When Demetrius got out of the rental car, he stretched and leaned against the front fender, facing the long verdant Tolland Green. Without moving, he scanned, working his way down both sides of the stately swath of grass dotted with towering mature trees, zigzagging from one side to the other. His survey drifted to front doors and front-facing facades and yards. His mind called up the names of occupants he associated with each house, remembering more than he had anticipated. He imagined that most, if not all, of the names he remembered were no longer connected to the houses he saw.

Demetrius didn't spend much time on any individual house along the Green until his view reached the far end of the meridian. A block or two beyond the end of the Green, where Mer-

2

row Road veered off toward Storrs and the interstate and Cider Mill Road angled off to the right and down the hill toward Crandell's Pond, there was a house in the triangle created by the split. He stared at that house intently, concentrating. He sorted through a treasury of memories, smiling at most and chuckling at some until he felt tears welling up.

After shaking himself free of the moment, Demetrius opened the trunk and extracted two bags—a suitcase and a cushioned laptop computer briefcase—and walked to the entrance to the large white Inn. On the ample wraparound porch, he turned and gazed once more at the house at the bottom of the Green before he went in. A bell tinkled when the door opened.

"You would be Mr. Clarke," Katherine Conrad said. "Four nights, a single, right?"

"Yes," Clarke replied. "Perhaps longer, perhaps not."

"We can make that work. I'll put you on the top floor if you don't mind the stairs. That way, you won't have to switch rooms when the weekend bookings arrive."

"Stairs are okay."

"Good. We've got your credit card in the system from when you booked with us. You want us to bill to that one?"

"Yes."

"Great. So, breakfast is from 6:30 'til 10. There's always coffee and lemonade in the sitting room. On weekend evenings, we have appetizers and wine there, too. If you need anything, just ask me or Jeff. He's in the backyard right now, finishing up some new lawn chairs—his own version of an Adirondack. He blends a Shaker sensibility into the traditional version, and it somehow makes the chairs more modern. It's odd how that works out, don't you think? Two old standards that somehow become modern when they meet each other.

Anyhow, Jeff's happy to have folks watch him work, so if you'd like to say hello—"

"No, thanks. Please just show me to the room."

Something in Demetrius's tone told Katherine that he wasn't in the mood for socializing. A trace of disappointment danced across her face, but her practiced smile replaced it almost immediately. "Yes indeedy-doo," she said. "Follow me, please."

Demetrius didn't have a lot to unpack. He used one dresser drawer for socks and underwear and shook out three button-down shirts, hanging them in the closet beside a pair of khakis and a pair of gray jeans. He left a few rolled-up polo and tee shirts and a bathing suit in the suitcase and laid the open case on the floor of the closet. His fold-up toiletry case had a loop at its top, and he hung it on the back of the bathroom door. Next, he took his laptop out of its case and placed it on a small round colonial table near the room's two windows, then found an outlet and fed power to the computer. He flipped it open to confirm that it was charging and then gently folded it shut again.

Demetrius sat in the small club chair beside the table and gazed out the window. He could see the three-street intersection at the top of the Green and, across the street from him, an antique shop that had once been a one-man Red & White grocery store. The transformation from grocery to antiques hadn't made significant changes to the structure's facade, which he found comforting. There had been a coin-operated soda pop cooler on the entry porch, featuring Coca-Cola graphics but containing other soft drinks as well, but it was gone. That change caused him to sigh. He also recognized the building directly across the street from him, although he had to squint to make out the sign in front of it; the town jail was now

4

a museum.

Demetrius decided to take a walk. It was growing warmer, so he shed his blazer and rolled up his sleeves before he left the room. He went out the front door of the Inn and turned right, taking the sidewalk between the road and the front yards of houses on one side of the Green. He passed the bank building and the church and the library, where signage indicated it was now Tolland's Town offices. He was passing in front of Zoey Caldwell's cottage, the smallest house on the Green, when he noticed the collection of vehicles in front of the house next door to the schoolhouse.

There was a Connecticut State Trooper cruiser, two nondescript black sedans, an ambulance, and a hearse. The ambulance had backed onto the front yard. Clarke saw a few people milling about near the front door and stopped walking. He watched for a moment or two and then deliberately turned away, crossing the street and the Green and turning back, headed for the antique store and the museum.

Nobody heard Demetrius Clarke say, "An ambulance, a hearse, and the cops. Not exactly the welcoming party I'd hoped for."

Chapter 2

"SO, DOCTOR KRASKIN, what can you tell us?"

Robert Kraskin looked from Art Shultz to Billy Williamson, then back to Shultz. Both men in front of him wore Connecticut State Trooper uniforms. Shultz's uniform had a lot of brass, Williamson's none.

"I can tell you that this man is dead," Kraskin said.

"No kidding," Shultz replied. "My nine-year-old coulda told me that."

"Yes, I imagine so," Kraskin said. "The signs are hard to miss."

"You got a smart mouth on you, Doc."

Billy Williamson took a small step forward. "We're looking for something more helpful, sir. Natural causes or . . . something else?"

"I can't say. His face is red, but he was sitting outside in the sun. For all we know, he might have been sunbathing all day yesterday, forgot his SPF. Other than that, you'll just have to wait for an autopsy." A small smile appeared. "But you can trust me on this much: autopsy's gonna say he's dead."

Shultz, his face stern, turned to Williamson. "We'll need permission for that, Billy. Have you talked to the family?"

"No, sir. Best I can tell, talking to the neighbors before you got here, there is no family. He lived alone."

Shultz pointed. "That's an awful lot of house for just one

fellow. No houseguests? Maybe that kid, the paperboy who found the body, knows something."

Kraskin smiled. "I bet you're not from around here, right?"

Shultz bristled, but before he could speak, Williamson leaned in and said, "Lieutenant Shultz is the day shift commander for Troop C, Doctor. We've got a lot of territory to cover. I'm assigned to Tolland, here full-time, but my chief—"

"Isn't one of us," the doctor said. He turned to face Shultz. "Let me put it to you this way: you know they say every village has its idiot?"

"Yeah."

"Well, we have a slightly different version. Ike Karas was our village SOB. Had a mean streak two miles wide, didn't socialize, didn't want to. He lived alone, and as far as most of us were concerned, that was no surprise. The only other time I dealt with him, he came to my office in Rockville with a minor infection from a cut on his arm. I cleaned it, treated it, bandaged him up. Spent maybe fifteen minutes with him. Total bill was 48 bucks."

"Yeah? So what?" Schultz's tone was sharp.

"He stiffed me, is what. Ducked four, five notices, wouldn't take our calls. My admin gal said we should just write it off, but I sent him to collection. I mean, everybody knows the guy paid for this house in cash, no mortgage, then spent a ton redoing everything: kitchen, wiring, paint, floor restoration, thermal windows, that spiffy deck. But he stiffed me for chump change. He treated everybody in town like that. All his contractors had to chase him for payment. You guys will probably find a whole lot of folks who'd be mighty happy to see Ike carved into pieces. But Billy's right that there's nobody who can sign off on an autopsy."

"Got it," Shultz confirmed. "Okay, Billy, you get on the

phone, check in with the legal eagles, see if we need a court order. Arrange it with Hartford once you sort out the paperwork. You know who to call?"

Williamson nodded and reached for his pants pocket. "Got all those contacts in my notepad, right here."

"Good. Get at it, then. Thanks for next to nothing, Doc. You can go now. We'll take care of transporting the body."

Kraskin picked up his bag. "You need me for anything else, I'll be in my Rockville office all day."

"Right. Billy, you make those calls, then canvass this whole street, see if anybody saw anything, heard anything. Grill that kid again, too."

"You think somebody killed Karas?" Williamson's face showed some anxiety.

"Well, I doubt it, but the doc wasn't any help about that," Shultz said. "No sign of a struggle, nothing out of place, and no marks on him I can see, so he sure as hell wasn't shot. I'm thinking it was his heart, but we have to find out, right?"

"*We?*"

"You. We're stretched thin, summer vacations and all, and I got a whole team working on that nutcase in Stafford Springs who whacked his parents and two neighbors. Plus, we got guys out on I-84 citing speeders, monitoring fender benders. If nobody marched in and strangled this guy, and I sure as hell hope that's the case, then it's not a crime, and we'll be done with it. But you're on your own."

"Yes, sir."

"Don't screw it up, rookie."

* * *

When Demetrius Clarke paused and looked back, the only vehicle still in sight from the earlier cluster was the cruiser. As he strolled, he saw a tall young man in uniform climb into it and pull away from the curb.

Demetrius was hungry. He'd nibbled at the boring meal they served on the plane, leaving most of it. He went to his room and grabbed his car keys. He pulled out of the parking area, turned left and then left again. The back road to Rockville rose and fell over hills, twisting a little here and there. He hadn't been on that road in decades, but he remembered it without hesitation. He recognized most of the houses he passed. There was a convenience store just after he turned away from the Green, which was new and shiny, but everything else was as it had been: wooded, quiet, sylvan. He knew without thinking where the intersections would be, when the curves would appear, and the view toward Rockville when he crested the last hill. He drove happily, comforted by a sense of belonging, which was so welcome that he motored along quite slowly to savor it.

Finding a storefront diner, Demetrius had a BLT and then walked around long enough to absorb all the changes that had come to the town. They were ample, but the place felt familiar despite the influx of chains and fast-food franchises and several shops that were in his memory bank but no longer on the streets. When he climbed out of the car, back in Tolland, the accumulated tension of a long flight, perfunctory airline service, and a grumpy car rental clerk no longer bunched his neck and shoulders.

Demetrius went up to his room and pulled a book out of a pocket in his computer bag. Then, he went back down the stairs and found a chair in the backyard, where he settled in, splitting his time between reading and remembering. His internal clock was so out of whack that he had no appetite for dinner. So, he spent the evening in his room, reading until he couldn't and sleeping through the night.

* * *

Breakfast was delicious, consisting of fluffy scrambled eggs, bacon or sausage, French toast, and, next to a toaster on the sideboard near the oversized dining table, rye and a white bread and English muffins. The coffee was excellent, too.

Katherine Conrad had everything so well planned and arranged that she sat and joined Clarke and the only other guest, a sales rep who offered a terse greeting and devoured food and a *Wall Street Journal* with equal zest. Jeff Conrad, wearing bib overalls over an ancient, faded red tee shirt, work boots, and a bandana around his neck, ambled in and poured coffee into a paper cup, pausing only long enough to give his guests a cursory nod and Katherine a perfunctory kiss.

"Lawn needs mowin'. Side flower gah-den weedin'. Tenny Baker comin' by. See you at lunch," Jeff said.

Jeff was out of the room before Katherine said, "See you then, dear." Then, she turned to Demetrius. "So, Mr. Clarke, do you have plans? They say it's going to be hot and humid today, so a visit to the pond might be nice. The day camp kids will be there, but if you pick the right spot on the beach, you can read and relax without getting trampled. I don't go often because there are always kids from the elementary school where I teach, and sometimes, their moms, too. So, it gets to be a little like work for me, and I like my summer vacation just as much as the kids do. Did I mention I teach third grade? If you feel like driving, I think there's a farmer's market in Vernon today; it's fun, lots of nice folks there, fresh produce and fruit. Then, of course, there's Old Sturbridge, just off the interstate on the way up to Boston."

"Thanks," Demetrius said, "but I have an appointment this morning."

"Really? How interesting! Business?"

"Not exactly. I'm going to have a chat with Ms. Bondurant."

"Bonnie? The real estate lady? She's lovely. She's in our book club. When her Daisy was in my class, Bonnie was a terrific mom, pitching in on projects, chaperoning field trips. I just love that name, Daisy, don't you? Just like the flower. She was one of my brightest. Are you planning to buy something here? If you are, Bonnie's the right choice. There's an agency in Rockville, and they handle some Tolland properties, too. But they don't know the area the way Bonnie does. She's a real go-getter.

"You're from Los Angeles, right?" Katherine continued. "That's the address you gave us when you booked. That would be quite a change, going from a huge city like that to our little village. I hear there's so much traffic there that you can hardly get anywhere. They say the weather's beautiful, but I think I'd go bonkers, so many people and all. I'm going to have just a splash more coffee. We've got three couples coming in for the weekend, and Lucinda's already up there prepping their rooms. A bit more coffee for you?"

Demetrius laid his hand over his mug. "I'm good, thank you."

"Okay." Katherine stood and moved to the coffee carafe. "Just a teensy bit more, you know, so I can keep up with Lucinda. She's a force to be reckoned with, that girl. I think it's 'cause she cleans for a lot of folks, so she doesn't have time to spare. But she's a real wizard, getting everything just right in a hurry. Your room's spotless, isn't it? Bathroom clean enough for surgery, sheets tight as a drum, am I right? Don't know how I'd get by without her, especially when school's in."

The sales rep lowered his paper and looked over his glasses at Katherine. He looked like he wanted to say something, but

11

he merely held her eyes.

"Good morning again, Mr. Sherman," Katherine greeted him. "Is your breakfast okay? There's one piece of French toast here. Why don't you polish it off so it doesn't go to waste?"

"Thank you, no," Sherman said. "I have to get going." He rose and moved rapidly out of the room, taking the stairs two at a time to get away.

"I should be going as well," Demetrius said. "I'd like to clean up and shave before my meeting." As he left the room, he glanced back. Katherine was sipping at her coffee, and she appeared to be talking to herself.

In jeans, a navy polo shirt, and a light tan driving cap, Demetrius Clarke strolled down the Green toward his meeting. The air was faintly damp, but the sky above was clear; there were some dark thunderheads in the far distance. Clarke lingered in front of the library, wondering if it still smelled like books since they'd added the town offices in back. When he turned to continue walking, he saw an elderly woman in the distance, slowly making her way toward him.

The approaching woman was using a walker, but it wasn't a typical one. It wasn't metal, and it didn't have tennis balls on its feet. Her walker was clearly handcrafted, all burnished wood, and it was tall. The woman gripped handlebars as she moved slowly forward, her arms level with her waist. She was using the walker for balance, but instead of being hunched over the thing, she stood straight and tall, her head held high. She was well-dressed, with a small beaded purse on her arm and a colorful wide-brimmed sun hat. The outfit, her posture, and the handsome walker gave her an air of elegance and command.

Demetrius resumed his stroll as the woman came toward him. When she was a few yards away, he stepped off the sidewalk and onto a front lawn, allowing her to pass without having to adjust her route. As she passed, he lifted his hat and nodded. "Good day, ma'am."

The woman nodded but didn't speak. Clarke moved back onto the sidewalk and took a couple of steps, then heard, "Just one moment, young man." Clarke stopped and turned. The woman had swiveled the walker around to face him. "I know you," she said.

"Ma'am?"

"Give me a moment, and it will come to me, I'm sure." The woman stared at him, her brow knit in concentration. "You're one of the summer people. You've grown! Everyone does, of course. But you used to be . . . oh, dear . . . you must think me daft . . ."

Demetrius smiled and took a step forward. "Mrs. Baker, isn't it? Sorry, I didn't recognize you. I am Demetrius Clarke. I used to spend summers just down the street."

"Yes!" Mrs. Baker exclaimed, beaming. "You're Beth Church's son. No, no, that's not right; Beth never married. Nephew? Yes, you're Beth's sister Victoria's boy. We called you Rusty."

Clarke nodded and smiled. "It wasn't Rusty. It was Rus-D. Nobody could figure out a nickname for Demetrius until my dad sort of glued parts of the end to the first letter—R-U-S and D. Rus-D. I haven't heard that in years."

"Are you staying with Beth?"

Demetrius took another step forward, removed his hat, laid it over his chest, and lowered his voice. "No, ma'am. Aunt Beth passed away some time ago. So did my parents. The house has been sold several times since then, I believe. I haven't been here in a long time."

The woman nodded, concentrating. "You're right, of course. I knew that. My memory . . . never mind. I liked Beth.

She was good Tolland folk. Victoria, too—she taught school here for a year or so, I seem to recall. Those girls, so pretty. They were named for queens, but you know that. Are you heading to the library? Walk with me?"

Demetrius smiled. "No, I'm going in the other direction."

"Ah, too bad. I have business with the town, so I'd best be on my way." Mrs. Baker started to turn the walker around, then hesitated. "You must come visit," she implored. "Do you remember which house?"

Demetrius smiled again. "Most certainly." He pointed across the street. "The large white house, next door to the old Town Hall. It has a huge backyard and a barn as well, I believe."

"I don't use that barn anymore. Fellow lives up toward Stafford Springs rents it from me. He stores old cars in it, can you imagine? Please do come by, will you? I'm not as spry as I once was, but I'll tell you this, young man, I can still out-bake anybody. Just made some apple cobbler yesterday. When shall I expect you?"

"I'm not sure, ma'am. Mid-morning, perhaps? I'll try to avoid all that food they serve at the Inn so that I have room for your cobbler. It will be delicious, I'm sure."

"You're staying there? Jeff Conrad's place? He made this walker. My father taught us to stand straight and look every person you meet in the eye. I looked at walkers in some shabby shop in Rockville, but I had to bend over to use them. I wasn't going to be one of those old folks, bent in half just to walk around—father certainly wouldn't approve. I told Jeff about it, and he understood. He built this contraption."

"It is an impressive piece of craftsmanship."

"He's very talented, Jeff is. His wife's a teacher, too, like your mom. Not quite the same, though."

"Oh?"

14

"No. Katherine is quite sweet, don't get me wrong, and one ought not speak ill, but . . . you may have noticed"—a tiny wicked grin appeared and vanished so quickly that Clarke almost missed it—"that woman can't be still for one second. My, how she goes on!"

Demetrius laughed. He extended his hand, and Mrs. Baker gripped it, her eyes fixed on his. "Good Tolland people," she said. "That's what you come from. Do come visit me."

"I promise."

* * *

"**T**his is it," Bonnie Bondurant said. Bonnie and Demetrius were standing on the shoulder of Cider Creek Road, facing the front door of the home. "Parish House."

Demetrius shook his head slowly. "We never called it that," he said. "It was just the house in Tolland. I always thought of it as Aunt Beth's house. Aunt Beth and my mom always called it 'mom and dad's farm.' It's in great shape."

"It's a jewel all right. 1730, give or take. Built for its namesake, Jeremiah Parish. Historic designation, of course. The floor plan is unchanged. The owners just had the exterior painted—I think that color, faded barn red, is just right for it. And I believe the roof is newer. Not sure about that date, but we can check on it."

"When I called, you said it isn't on the market," Clarke said.

"It's definitely not," Bonnie confirmed. "I'd know even if they listed it with that franchise operation over in Rockville. I sold it to them in the first place, so if they were selling, I hope they'd list it with me. He teaches over at UConn, and she stays home with their kid—sweet little girl, four? No, six years old now. I believe she does something for a New York company. I can't quite recall what, but she works from home, so she's always with the little one. I see them now and then; they love the house."

"There is much to love," Demetrius said. "Looks like they use the front door as the main entrance. We never did. We'd come and go using the back door off the kitchen porch or the side door on the other side, facing the other street. There were window boxes on that side, filled with Morning Glories. My grandmother loved her gardens, and the house was white then, so you couldn't miss those flowers. I don't think I ever once used this door, but I remember the hallway it opens onto is dark, no windows. When I was little, it seemed a bit scary to me—not threatening, just a little spooky."

"How long did you live here?"

"Well, we lived in Maryland, close to DC. This was the summer place, so I didn't really live here; Aunt Beth did with my grandmother until my grandmother died. My mom and I would come up a few weeks after school let out and spend most of the summer here. My Dad had to work, but he always managed to get a couple of weeks off, and he'd sneak in long weekends, too. I don't remember being a toddler here, but I know I was. Came back every year until I was in my early teens."

Bonnie listened intently, watching Demetrius with a gently calculating eye. "You have a history here, then," she said. "That's nice. As I say, this one isn't on the market, but I've got several others. Nothing on the Green—at least not right now. But I suspect a particularly attractive house to come on the market soon."

"The one next door to the schoolhouse?"

"Yes. Fellow who lived there died quite suddenly, just yesterday. How did you know?"

"I saw all the emergency vehicles and guessed. It's sort of an occupational hazard."

"Oh? You're a cop?"

Demetrius smiled. "Hardly. I'm a writer. Among other things, I write mysteries."

"Really? How interesting. Anything I've read?"

"I doubt it. I write them, they get published, and they get good reviews, but they don't sell a lot."

Bonnie's sales acumen kicked in. "Well, then, I guess I have to ask. The prices around here are still reasonable, but the best places can be . . ."

Demetrius turned and faced her. "I've recently come into a windfall. Hardly millionaire territory, mind you. But I've done some research on my own, and I'm confident I could afford to buy here."

Bonnie's smile was enthusiastic.

"If I . . . chose to do so," Demetrius added.

Bonnie noted the hesitant tone. "I can show you several properties—good, solid homes, and some with great views."

Demetrius shook his head. "Not yet," he said.

Bonnie pointed to the front door. "Is it this one, then, or none at all?"

"I don't know," Demetrius said. "As I say, it's too soon."

"I could certainly ask them, the current owners, I mean, if they have any interest in selling."

Demetrius shook his head. "That might mislead them. I'm just not sure yet. Best not to give them false hope, I think. But there is something you could do for me, if it's convenient."

"Of course."

"I'd love to *see* the property. The backyard, the gardens," Demetrius pointed to their right, "those enormous pine trees. The grown-ups used to have cocktails under those trees. There was a large wooden shed at the back end of the property, open-air, with a garage. The garage must have been built for a carriage, but Aunt Beth could fit her Chevy in it."

"It's still there," Bonnie said.

"I'm glad. If it isn't too much of an intrusion, maybe they'd let me come in and browse around? That would be wonderful."

"I could give them a call and ask."

"Please do."

"You're staying at the Inn?"

"Yes."

"I'll get in touch, leave a message with Katherine."

"Thank you."

"My pleasure," Bonnie said. "I'm sorry, but I have another appointment. I must dash off, but I'll definitely be in contact."

"Don't let me keep you," Demetrius said.

Bonnie walked toward her car. As she pulled the door open, she glanced back. Demetrius Clarke was still standing on the entry walk, staring at the house. Bonnie prided herself on her ability to read her clients, but this one perplexed her. She sensed something—was it loss? Sadness? Loneliness? She wondered if he was actively looking for a home or just indulging in a nostalgic fantasy.

Chapter 3

THE WEEKEND GUESTS had arrived at the Inn. When Demetrius walked into the living room, Katherine Conrad took his arm and led him to a sideboard that held a cheese platter, tiny hot dogs in a reddish sauce, lemonade, and several bottles of wine. She turned to face the other guests. "Everyone, this is Mr. Clarke," she announced.

A young couple, seated close to one another on a sofa, waved. A woman with short graying hair smiled and took the hand of the man standing beside her chair. "I'm Jenny," she said, "and this is my husband, Rob. These young folks are Diane and Hank. They're just married."

"Good evening," Demetrius said. He paused and then added, "I'm Rus-D."

Katherine said, "The toothpicks in the shot glass are for these little sausages. The sauce is spicy, but not too. The cheeses are from a sweet little shop in Rockville. The wine came from there, too. I made the lemonade this afternoon, so it's fresh. The Kents—those youngsters—are on a New England road trip for their honeymoon. Jenny and Rob are from Boston. They come down now and then to escape city life. Mr. Clarke is here all the way from Los Angeles."

Rob took a hefty gulp of his wine and moved to refill his glass. "LA, eh?" he said. "You involved in Hollywood? I'm head producer of a Boston TV news operation. Always wanted to get out to your town and visit a studio, see how they make the magic."

Demetrius didn't respond immediately. His expression grew dark briefly, and he turned away from the group for a moment, slowly slicing a wedge of cheese. While Rob filled his glass, Demetrius said, "I had a brush with the business recently, but no, thankfully, I'm not 'involved.'"

"Too bad," Rob said. "Thought maybe I could score a private tour or something."

"Like we'll ever get out there," Jenny said. "I'm a labor attorney. Between my practice and the fact that Rob's station can't get through a day without him, we don't get much time off. Little trips like this one are the best we can do."

Demetrius nodded, pointing to his mouth and shrugging as he worked on a hunk of cheese.

The young couple asked Katherine to recommend a place where they could get dinner. Katherine dashed over to the registration desk, grabbed a sheet of paper, and handed it to them. "Here's a list," she said. "You'll find stars next to my favorites and driving directions under each place. It depends on how far you want to drive and what you're in the mood for, but I think you'll find something suitable somewhere. Jenny, don't you and Rob have a favorite spot?"

While the five of them chatted energetically about dining, Demetrius drifted over to the windows at the back of the room and stared at the backyard. He was relieved that nobody had pursued his "brush with Hollywood" story, and he spent a few moments forcing himself to enjoy the view as a means of driving that from his mind. His concentration was broken when the front door opened and its bells chimed.

The tall young police officer who had been standing on the lawn in front of the house beside the school entered the Inn. He was in his uniform, his trooper hat in his hand at his side. "Good evening," he said.

Katherine scurried over and gave the officer a welcoming hug. "Billy Williamson," she said, "whatever brings you here? Am I under arrest? That would be exciting, although I can't imagine what I might have done. Can I offer you some lemonade? A snack? If you're off duty, we have wine, too. Please do come in."

Williamson seemed a bit thrown by Katherine's enthusiasm, but he smiled at her. "No wine, thanks. I'm sorry to intrude, but I need to speak with—"

"Jeff? He's in his shed. There's something wrong with the lawn mower, and he's determined to fix it so he can finish mowing the backyard first thing tomorrow. You know where the shed is, don't you? Out that door, back in the corner of the yard. Don't be upset if he's cranky with you. That mower gives him problems all the time, and he gets quite out of sorts with it. If he's short with you, it's nothing personal. Would you like me to call him? I can holler out the door, and he usually hears me."

Williamson looked confused. "No, Ms. Conrad. I'm not here for Jeff. It's one of your guests I need to—"

"Oh, dear," Katherine interrupted. "Is it bad news?"

"No, ma'am." Williamson stepped around Katherine and faced the group. "I'd like to have a word with Mr. Clarke, please. Is one of you—"

"*I'm* Demetrius Clarke."

The officer nodded and walked over to the windows where Clarke stood. Williamson offered his hand, and Demetrius shook it. "I'm sorry to interrupt your evening," Williamson said, "but I think you may be able to help me with a problem. I sure hope so."

"I'm sorry," Clarke said. "I don't have any idea what you're talking about."

Williamson turned and faced the others in the room, all of whom were watching and listening with rapt attention. "Could we just step outside, sir?" he asked, turning back to Demetrius. "Maybe sit on the porch for a few minutes? I'd really be grateful."

Katherine Conrad stepped forward. "Is Mr. Clarke in trouble, Billy? He's only been here a day or so, you know, and nothing out of the ordinary has— I mean, he hasn't . . . I'd be amazed if he . . . surely, you can't think that he . . ."

Williamson held up a hand to quiet Katherine. "Ms. Conrad, please. There's nothing wrong. I just want to ask Mr. Clarke some questions, is all." He turned to Demetrius again. "The front porch, sir? Or we could take a walk around the backyard. I promise not to take much time."

Demetrius, as confused as he was curious, nodded. "Let's sit on the porch," he said and led the way to the front door.

Billy carried his hat and a cup of lemonade, Demetrius his wine. They settled onto a wicker sofa facing the Green. The thunderheads Demetrius noticed earlier had now drifted past the town, but the air was heavy and thick.

"I know this is pretty unusual," Billy Williamson began, "but I think you may be able to help me."

"I can't image how," Demetrius said, frowning.

"A fellow has died. Just down the street there. They found his body yesterday morning. I believe you were on the sidewalk when our investigation was getting started."

Demetrius twisted a little and looked directly at the officer. "You saw me?"

"I did."

"And remembered me."

"I was a little amped up, I guess. I didn't want to miss anything. The other officer, the guy standing with me, is my boss. I didn't want to . . . I didn't want him to think I wasn't paying attention."

"Impressive," Demetrius said. "But I don't see how I fit—"

"You write about crime, don't you?"

Demetrius was openly stunned. "How the hell . . ."

Williamson grinned. "When people talk about Tolland being a small town, sir, they aren't kidding. Everybody knows just about everybody else. And chatter—you know, the latest gossip—moves around at warp speed."

Demetrius thought for a moment. "Bonnie Bondurant."

Billy grinned again. "Roger that. Ran into her at that convenience store, the one just around the corner there, earlier today. We were getting coffee. She'd heard about Karas—he's the guy the paperboy found dead yesterday—and she figured I might be investigating what happened to him."

"And she told you—"

"Yes. She said you write mysteries, gave me your name."

"Well, yes, I've written a few, but . . ."

Billy leaned forward. "I'm going to be honest with you, sir. I've been in Tolland less than a year. It's my first assignment. I did well on the exams and in training, and Art Shultz—he's my boss—took an interest in me. He got the brass to assign me to Troop C—that's his turf. He says I could be a good cop."

Demetrius nodded. "But not yet?"

Billy smiled. "Not yet. Mostly, I deal with petty thefts and traffic violations and fender benders. I patrol the town, keep an eye on things, and get called out now and then when families go off the rails—kids acting out, guy gets a little too physical with the wife, that sort of thing. It's all pretty tame. Karas is my first death."

23

"It wasn't . . . is it a *murder*?"

"We don't know. Won't know until we get the autopsy results, probably not until Monday. Art thinks the guy probably went out with a bad ticker, something like that."

"And you?"

"I'm not so sure. Like I say, it's a small town, and this guy, Karas, he wasn't exactly Mr. Congeniality, you know? He had a way of rubbing everybody the wrong way. Arrogant SOB. Mostly petty stuff, but he could be rude, even mean. And he's kicked off a couple of loud confrontations. I'm hoping Art's right, but if he's not, then I'm looking down the barrel of a murder."

The officer's eyes drifted around the Green for a moment before he continued. "If it is murder, Mr. Clarke, I'm not sure . . . well, that's a big deal, right? I'd sure like to be able to do my job, but I haven't done any investigations like this—not one. I'm not . . . I don't have a lot of confidence, truth be told."

"And you think, what? You think my work makes me—"

"I'm hoping that a guy who spends his time dreaming up mysteries would, I don't know, have some insights? Your books, they involve murder?"

"Yes, but—"

"So, you've spent way more time than I have thinking about killing. I mean, I know about the basics, you know: means, motive, opportunity. That was part of our training. But if this is the real deal . . ." Williamson brought his gaze back and fixed his eyes on Demetrius's. "If this is the real deal, sir, I'm going to need all the help I can get."

Clarke was touched by the sincerity of the plea. He was also amused, and a small laugh escaped before he could squelch it.

Billy winced. "Please, sir . . ."

Demetrius laid a hand on the young man's shoulder. "I'm

sorry, I'm laughing at myself, not you. I don't think I can offer much. For one thing, I'm only here for a few days. If it *is* murder, your work will take a lot longer than that. And for another, I make everything up. I write fiction, officer, not true crime."

"I get that, but what I know about murder wouldn't spill out of a thimble. All I'm asking is, can you help me sort out what I learn, maybe keep me pointed in the right direction? I'd hate to muck this up. It's pretty much make or break for me."

"There's one more thing," Demetrius said. "You couldn't have picked a lousier time to ask."

"Oh?"

Demetrius sighed and shifted his gaze to his shoes. "I'm not in very good shape right now, officer. My career is floundering, I'm not happy with my work. I've just escaped an ugly little corner of hell. I'm a fugitive from my own life right now. I'm here because I need some time to figure out what I'm doing. I don't know where I belong, and I don't know where I'm going. Even if I could help, and I'm not saying I can, my judgment is no better than shaky. You need somebody solid, reliable, and focused. I'm none of that."

The two men sat in silence. Clarke was embarrassed and surprised by his candor. Williamson was taken aback by what he'd heard and had no sense of how to atone for having triggered it.

Clarke drained his wine glass and stood. "I'm sorry, Officer Williamson. I just don't think I'm the man for the job."

"Yeah. I'm afraid that makes two of us."

Demetrius chuckled. "Sondheim: 'Isn't it rich, aren't we a pair?'"

"Sounds 'bout right," Billy said, smiling. "I'm sorry to have bothered you." Williamson rose and put on his hat, adjusting it so it was just right. "Thanks for your time. I hope you have a pleasant evening." He turned to go down the steps. His shoulders slumped, and his gait was slow.

Demetrius watched the officer leave and felt miserable. "Officer Williamson, wait." Williamson turned to face him. "If you get the autopsy report on Monday, look me up. I'll listen to what you know. No promises, mind you."

Williamson grinned. "Everyone calls me Billy. And you got a deal."

Chapter 4

DEMETRIUS SLEPT LATE on Saturday morning. When he came downstairs, Katherine was nowhere to be seen, and the dining room table had been cleared. He went to the living room and found a carafe, poured himself a cup of coffee, and took it to the front porch. He sat on the bench where he and Officer Williamson had talked and watched Tolland. The sky was cloudless, and the humidity of the previous evening had vanished.

The antique shop across the street was open, and a woman was sweeping the entry porch. There was a fellow riding a lawn mower in the large front yard of one of the big houses off to Demetrius's left, on the upper portion of the Green. The man leaned out to one side of the machine to make sure his lines were straight. The mower was far enough away that its noise was muted to a metallic hum; otherwise, the town was quiet and calm.

At the other end of the Green, between the schoolhouse and the old Town Hall, some people were setting up umbrellas and pop-up canopies. A group of cars lined the street, and folks were removing boxes and crates from trunks and back seats and carrying them to portable tables sporting plastic gingham covers.

"That's our swap meet," Katherine said, standing directly behind Demetrius. "Every other week, all summer long."

Demetrius hadn't heard the door open, never mind Katherine's approach. He was startled enough to spin around, spilling a little coffee onto his shoes and the porch floor.

"Oh, dear," Katherine said. "I'm afraid I scared you. I'm so sorry. I'll get a rag. Did you get coffee on your slacks? If you did, bring them to me, and I'll have Lucinda wash them, first thing. Jeff always tells me to stop sneaking up on him, but it's not on purpose. I just don't make much noise when I move around, I guess. Honestly, I'm not being sneaky or anything. I didn't mean to startle you. Please forgive me."

"It's okay, Ms. Conrad. It's just a little coffee, and these loafers are my knock-around shoes. They've endured worse. You might want to sop up the floor, though, so the whitewash doesn't stain."

Katherine backed away and went into the kitchen, returning rapidly with a tattered kitchen towel. She sopped up the drops on the floor and offered the rag to Demetrius. "You sure the shoes are okay, Mr. Clarke? I'd hate to ruin them. I don't know about you, but I do love a good pair of shoes. You know, comfortable without being too tight, good enough to wear in company. I wear sneakers when I'm at school. I'm on my feet most of the time, but by the time the day ends, it's a relief to get off my feet, I can tell you that. Can I get you some more coffee?"

Demetrius shook his head and rose. "No, thanks. I was planning to take a long walk, so I'll just leave this cup with you and push off."

Demetrius crossed the street and stood in front of the antique store, admiring the vintage Red & White sign hanging on the porch wall. He debated going in but chose not to, thinking there would be time enough to browse later or another day. He turned and began walking slowly down the sidewalk toward the swap meet. He paused in front of each house as he strolled.

The first house, next to the antique shop, was one of the few in town that was impersonal to Demetrius. It was fenced and gated and hidden behind tall, lush shrubs. Not once during his summers in Tolland had he seen anyone come or go from it. He'd always thought of it as a curious place, maybe even mysterious, and he found it reassuring that it remained so.

Demetrius knew the next house well: the Banks family. A set of grandparents were year-round residents, and their children and grandchildren, all from New Jersey, spent every summer there. The sprawling house had an enormous flat backyard, which was a summer social center, the site of evening cocktail parties, smaller picnics, potluck gatherings, and, on one occasion, a lawn bowling tournament that, to Demetrius's annoyance, had been for grown-ups only. Tolland had been about a third as large then as it was now, and in his memory, it seemed that everyone who lived there, including the summer people, had been in that yard, sometimes all at once.

Demetrius couldn't recall the name of the elderly couple in the next house down, but he remembered visiting the house with Aunt Beth and his mother—visits that usually included the delivery of a pie or a container of berries or flowers from his grandmother's garden. The couple living there had seemed ancient to him. He calculated that the house had welcomed new occupants more than once in the intervening years.

The Flynn house was next. "Pint" Flynn, an enormous, round, jolly fellow, was an executive with Pratt & Whitney and the chief of the Tolland Volunteer Fire Department. His wife and two kids—a brother and sister—were popular and deeply connected to Tolland's goings-on. Pint—derived from his high school nickname, Half Pint, bestowed because he was anything but—sat on his front porch every evening with a beer, waving to or chatting with anyone who happened by in the dusky fading sunlight.

On one hot summer Saturday, a brush fire had broken out on vacant land down the street from Parish House, and the firefighters, and most of the neighbors, had arrived in force. It wasn't much of a fire, but it was indelible for Demetrius because Pint had approached him, carrying a broom, and said, "Use this, Rus-D, on that little patch by the road. Beat the flames 'til they can't breathe."

"Flames" had been a modest exaggeration, but Rus-D had eagerly taken the broom and hammered away at smoldering scrub grass. Rus-D had been so proud that he beamed. Demetrius still felt a bit of pride recalling the incident.

Tenny—for Hortense—Baker was next on the block. She and her husband were Tolland leaders—he on the Town Council for ages, she organizing one fundraising or social event after another. It seemed to Rus-D that Tenny visited Aunt Beth and his mom several times a week, working on some project, soliciting—or demanding—assistance. In those days, Rus-D thought Tenny to be stern and a bit overbearing, and he'd once heard Aunt Beth call her "bossy."

The flower beds on both sides of the entrance to Tenny's house were immaculate and in full bloom. Demetrius imagined that Tenny Baker's demeanor held full sway over the yard: no blade of grass or weed dared grow anywhere near those flowers.

Demetrius turned and watched the swap meet on the Green in front of the old Town Hall. There were at least a dozen vendors, and most seemed practiced, their wares laid out in boxes that could easily be transported from this location to the next or back to a garage or basement. Two stalls were more commercial, with professional banners, countertop literature in sleeves, and corporate products artfully displayed—one offering cosmetics, the other weight loss products. The rest of the vendors were less polished. One man had boxes of CDs, magazines, and vintage toys. He was next to a woman offering sketches in cardboard frames. A few vendors offered a hodgepodge of household goods: pots and pans, glassware, recipe books, and more. The local PTA was selling cookies to raise funds next to tables laden with homegrown fruits, vegetables, jellies, and jams.

There was a woodworker in the mix, selling handsome handcrafted pieces: coasters, trays, smooth carved animals. He displayed an open notebook of furniture designs "built to your specifications."

Demetrius happily wandered among the stalls. It was a comfortable and unhurried event. Most were obviously neighbors, extending warm greetings to one another using first names. Several moms sent their children off to play on the Green: an enthusiastic game of tag, kickball, soccer practice, and exuberant running. The moms and the kids were equally at ease in their small-town security blanket.

Demetrius was leafing through the woodworker's portfolio when a cruiser pulled up in front of Ike Karas's house across the street. He watched Billy Williamson walk to the side of the house and out of sight, presumably going to inspect the teak patio once again.

The woodworker swiveled around and watched. He snorted. "Why bother?"

"Are you talking about that cop car?" Demetrius asked.

"Yeah," the woodworker confirmed. "Only point in investigating that man's death would be to give somebody a medal."

"You think it was murder?"

"Who cares? Heart attack, knife in the back, slashed throat, it all comes down to the same thing, doesn't it? Good riddance

31

to bad rubbish. You interested in any of those dining tables? Take my card." He pulled a business card from a streamlined wooden holder on the table. On the front, it said: *Mark Wells Interior & Exterior Woodwork, Cabinetry & Designer Furniture.* Demetrius flipped it over and saw *Tolland Town Council* printed above contact information.

"I'm from out of town," Demetrius said. "This table is wonderful, but shipping it across the country would cost me more than the table."

Wells grinned. "No problem, pal. I'll just jack the price up so they balance out."

Demetrius laughed.

"Where you from?" Wells asked.

"Los Angeles."

"Tinseltown. What brings you here?"

"Just a visit. Taking a little time for myself. I used to visit here every summer, wanted to see it all again. It hasn't changed much."

"We work hard to keep it that way," Wells said. "It's a good place to live." He thumbed toward the Karas house. "No thanks to guys like that."

"You're the second person who's told me he wasn't a good neighbor. I've been away a long time, but it's hard to imagine living here and not wanting to get along. It's so congenial here."

"New Yorkers," Wells said, the sneer in his voice unmistakable. "Too much money, too pushy, too damn sure they're always right. That guy was so rich—something to do with Wall Street, I hear. He figured he was entitled, thought he could muscle his way to whatever he wanted. His money, his rules, to hell with the rest of us."

"Sounds unpleasant," Demetrius agreed.

"Yeah. Just ask the Antonio family. They'd been renting over in Manchester, but Sarah, the wife, grew up here, and they scrimped and saved so they could move back. They worked with Bonnie—that's Bonnie Bondurant, the real estate gal here. They borrowed half the down-payment from Sarah's folks, scraped the rest together, and got all the paperwork squared away. They were all set to sign the contract."

"I've met Bonnie," Demetrius said. "So, what happened?"

"Karas happened. He shows up one day, says he's gonna retire early—guy's no more than forty-five, mind you, and he's already so rich he can quit—and he sees the *For Sale* sign over there, got Bonnie's number on it. Calls her, and she tells him it's about to go into escrow. He asks how much. She tells him, and he says, 'Add a hundred grand to that and make the offer.'

"Well, Bonnie wouldn't lie to the folks selling the place, so she takes 'em the offer. And, of course, they jump on it. Sarah and Bobby—he's her husband—never had a prayer once Karas started throwing money around. Far as I know, they're still renting."

"LA's like that," Demetrius said. "People spending more than they should because they can. I guess the difference in LA is that they tear down what they buy as soon as the deal closes so they can build something bigger. At least this guy didn't do that."

Wells snorted. "Not for lack of trying. He wanted to level the place so he could throw up some steel and glass monstrosity. On the Green! Filed paperwork for it, got denied—that beauty is historic, after all. And then he fought us tooth and nail for two years with lawyers, accountants, zoning specialists. He even hired a political outfit to try to run us out of office, but that didn't work, either. He finally gave up. But before he was done, he'd made enough enemies to fill Crandell's Pond."

A woman walked up to the table. Demetrius made a show of putting the business card in his pocket and stepped aside. "Mark," the woman said, "we're having trouble with that drain: the one on the corner in front of our house. It keeps backing up, floods the intersection. We've been complaining about it for weeks, but nothing ever happens. Can you help?"

"Sure, Katie," Wells agreed. "Email me the address, and I'll talk to the guys who take care of this stuff for us. Nothing happens, you get right back to me, okay?"

"Super," Katie said. "Thanks."

Demetrius lingered at the swap meet, enjoying the summer air and the sense of community for a while before he walked back to the Inn. He changed into a swimsuit, threw on an oversized soft corduroy surfer shirt, folded his paperback into a towel from the bathroom, and went to his car. He drove the short distance to the convenience store on the road to Rockville and bought a refrigerated tuna sandwich, a bag of chips, and a soda. He drove back to the Inn, parked the car, and set out afoot for Crandell's Pond. There were several newer houses lining the road below the Green, in between older ones he knew well. The smell of the sun-softened tar on the road was so familiar that it made him smile as he walked.

The sun had grown quite warm, and the parking lot was full. There were several families underneath a large wooden portico covering long picnic tables. A quartet of middle-aged men played tennis on one of the two courts near the parking area. The covered picnic area and the courts were unfamiliar to Demetrius, but the beach at the foot of the pond was as he remembered it.

Demetrius found a spot, unfurled his towel, removed his shirt, and sat. He set his book aside and unwrapped his sandwich. Nibbling at the tuna and chips, sipping the soda, he watched the pond. There was a small dam near Cider Mill Road, old and water-worn, where a group of teens was assembled, chattering and taking turns diving off the edge of the dam. Closer to him, smaller children frolicked in the shallower water by the beach while attentive adults watched and chatted. Further out, a couple of swimmers were churning along, executing what passed for laps.

Demetrius's gaze drifted to the far side of the pond, where a house—he remembered it as Lily Crandell's home—sat. One summer, Demetrius had taken a Red Cross swimming course, the final exam for which had been a distance swim. He had completed that challenge, following his instructor in a rowboat to a reedy area just below the house and back, all the way across the pond and back again. He had earned a patch to be affixed to his swimsuit. He had long since lost it, but the memory of meeting the challenge was clear and captivating.

After finishing his lunch, Demetrius stretched out, opening his book. In a matter of minutes, he dozed. He drifted in and out, the amorphous hum of children at play and conversations at a distance lulling him until a shadow and a voice directly above him intruded.

"I don't mean to be rude," a woman's voice said, "but I noticed you don't have any sunscreen on. You're going to burn if you're not careful."

Demetrius sat up and squinted at the woman.

"Sorry," the woman said, "but I don't recognize you, so I'm guessing you're a visitor here. We'd hate for you to end up all burned and sore. We want our visitors to be happier than that."

"We?"

"Tolland folk," the woman said, extending her hand and smiling. "I'm Pam Throop. I sit on the Town Council, and I'm in charge of our tourism campaign. You know, making sure people know what a special place we have here. It just wouldn't do, you telling everyone the only thing you got here was a wicked sunburn."

They shook hands.

"Demetrius Clarke, Ms. Throop. You're right; I didn't think to bring sunscreen." He unrolled the shirt he'd been using as a headrest and slipped into it. "I promise not to tell a soul if I've gotten too red."

Pam laughed. "Mission accomplished, then. What brings you to Tolland?"

"I knew it as a child. I'm getting reacquainted. I thought it would be relaxing to come back here, escape the big city for a while. I'm from LA."

"Good to meet you, Mr. Clarke. How are you finding our little village?"

"There seem to be more people here, and there are more homes along Cider Mill Road than I remember. But other than that, it hasn't changed very much at all. I see little changes here at the pond, but it's still a wonderful spot."

"Yes, it is," Pam agreed. "We're pretty big on conserving what we have here: protecting the historic properties, making sure our community stays connected to our heritage."

"I approve, for whatever that's worth. I was talking to one of your colleagues this morning, a Mr. Wells. He told me you stopped somebody from tearing down one of the houses on the Green."

"Mr. Karas," Pam said. "That was some fight. He just died the other day, and I'm already hearing from folks who want to make sure that house won't be razed or altered when it changes hands."

"He wasn't exactly a good neighbor, I gather."

"That's generous. Did Mark tell you he mounted a campaign to get us thrown off the Council?"

"He mentioned it."

"He hired some big deal political PR agency out of DC. They did a little sniffing around and found out that most folks here were perfectly happy with the Council. Our elections are usually contested, but the core values of Tolland don't change when somebody leaves and somebody else comes in. I know it sounds sort of wimpy, but Tolland politics are gentle—we don't have big fights 'cause we're all pretty much on the same page. Or, we were until Karas got involved."

"What happened?"

"The incumbents who stopped his plan to demolish his house—I was one of them—campaigned the way we always do. You know, lawn signs, neighborhood meet-and-greets, a town meeting for a debate. We're all neighbors, after all, so it's pretty much a family affair. But everybody started getting flyers and letters in the mail from something called 'Friends of Tolland.' One flyer accused Mark Wells of voting against Karas's plan because Karas wouldn't hire him to work on the new place he wanted to build—called it a conflict of interest. Sheer nonsense, of course. Mark wouldn't work for that guy on a prayer or a bet. But that didn't stop them from spreading it around."

"And you? Did they attack you as well?"

"I'll say! 'Friends of Tolland' sent flyers around claiming we live in Hartford, implying we bought our Tolland house just so I could get on the Council. I believe the phrase was 'Stop outsiders from destroying Tolland.'"

"I assume that's not true."

"The Hartford address they cited is Adrian's office—he's a CPA. It's an office tower, for heaven's sakes. Nobody lives there. Nevertheless, I had to keep reminding everybody that we've lived here for nearly ten years and that our kids go to school here. My neighbors see me every day, and even they asked me about it."

"But you're still on the Council, aren't you?"

"Sure am. Won easily, and so did Mark. Still, everybody in town heard I'm a liar and Mark's a cheat, and they heard it almost every day. The 'Friends' sure had plenty of money, and, big surprise, it all came from Ike Karas."

"Fascinating," Demetrius said.

"I suppose. You'd be hard-pressed to find anybody who thinks Karas was a good neighbor, that's for sure. Sorry to say so, but I think most folks don't feel like his death is the worst thing that ever happened here." Something at the edge of the pond distracted Pam. "Uh-oh, that's my little one over there scrapping with Denise's boy. I'd better go break that up before somebody starts bawling. Nice to meet you, Mr. Clarke."

"Likewise."

Demetrius stood, shed his shirt, and walked down to the water. He waded in slowly and then dove under. The water was so cold that it startled him. He treaded for a second, surprised that his memory of endless afternoons in the pond had somehow omitted the shock of its iciness. Then, he began swimming toward the center of the pond, working at it to warm up.

Chapter 5

"TELL US ABOUT your books," Katherine Conrad implored.

The guests were gathered in the living room. The tiny hot dogs had been supplanted by mini-squares of pizza. A salami and a slicing knife had been added to the cheese platter. Demetrius had a glass in one hand and a wine bottle in the other, but he didn't pour. Instead, he stared at Katherine. "Forgive me," he said, "but I'm quite sure I haven't mentioned . . ."

Katherine smiled. "You told Bonnie you're a writer, and Bonnie told Billy Williamson and the young lady he's dating—Carol something, I think? She was right in front of me in line at the grocery store in Rockville earlier today, and we got to chatting, and—"

"Got it," Demetrius said. "Small town."

Rob, the news producer, asked, "Fiction? Nonfiction? Poetry, maybe?"

"Bonnie says mysteries," Katherine supplied. "Is that right?"

"Yes," Demetrius said.

Hank, the new groom, said, "Mysteries. Huh. That why the cop came after you last night? We thought maybe you'd, like, ripped off a bank or something, didn't we, hon?"

Diane blushed. "Not really. You don't look like a criminal to me, Mr. Clarke. But it did seem odd, the police questioning you."

"I can guess," Jenny said. "That cop looks like he's about nineteen years old. I bet he wanted somebody who knows something about crime to, what, mentor him? Teach him?"

Katherine moved to stand next to Demetrius. "Carol says Billy's hoping that if Ike Karas—he's the guy down the street who died just before the rest of you checked in—was murdered, Mr. Clarke here can help him figure out whodunit. Golly, I've never said 'whodunnit' when it meant Who Done It for real! Of course, it should be who *did* it, not done it. But still, kind of exciting, don't you think?"

"So, you write mysteries?" Rob asked.

Demetrius filled his glass, sliced off some salami, and popped it in his mouth, washing it down with a robust slug of wine. "Yes, that's what I do."

"Murders?"

"Three are murder mysteries. Another one looks like a murder but turns out to be something else. In between, I write short stories about crimes other than murder and occasional freelance articles."

Jenny had her phone in her hand. "Rob, check this out." She was in a chair, and her husband stepped over and leaned in.

"What is— Oh, that's him, huh? Wow, five stars for three of them, 4.8 for the other. That's impressive. You must be a best seller with ratings like that."

Demetrius gave an exaggerated shake of his head. "Not a chance, Rob. Unless your name is Grisham or King, you don't make much money. I get modest sales, but I spent a good deal of time in a law firm before I started writing, so I've got savings to keep me going, at least for a while. If I lived on book sales, I'd be eating ramen most of the time."

"Is that why you're moving to Tolland?" Katherine asked.

Demetrius stared directly at her, his gaze as gentle as he

could make it. "I have no specific plan to move here," he said, "no matter what Bonnie says."

Katherine blushed. "I'm so sorry," she said. "I didn't mean to—"

Demetrius waved her off. "It's okay, Ms. Conrad. Sorry if I snapped. Truth is, I have no plan at all. I'm kind of wandering around at the moment. And wandering to Tolland seemed like a good idea."

"So, why was that cop after you?" Hank asked.

"Jenny's right, more or less. He's young, and he's concerned that if this Karas man was murdered, he's not up to the investigation. He thought maybe I could help him."

"Will you?"

"I've agreed to talk with him on Monday. Nothing more than that."

"What are you working on now?" Jenny asked. "Another murder or something else?"

"Nothing," Demetrius said. "I don't have a current project."

"Writer's block?"

"No. I've just been through a difficult stretch, and I . . ." Demetrius paused and considered. "No, forget that. I'm just on a little vacation, clearing away the cobwebs." He took a sip of wine and turned to Rob. "So, you do evening news, Rob? Not the morning fill-ins for the network, but the primetime slots?"

They all chatted for another half-hour and then scattered, the newlyweds to a movie, Rob and Jenny to a concert in Hartford. Demetrius drove the few miles from Tolland to Storrs, where he strolled the streets surrounding the UConn campus and found a bar-bistro for dinner.

* * *

On Sunday, after a breakfast that featured ample portions of rich choices that Katherine served with an endless parade of stories, observations, and opinions, the guests scattered. Demetrius took a coffee and his book into the Inn's backyard and settled into one of Jeff Conrad's homemade lawn chairs. There were a variety of birds in the trees surrounding the yard, and they chirped continuously. Jeff Conrad was in his work shed, a sizable and well-organized space, sawing, hammering, and sanding. The competing noises made reading with concentration difficult, so Demetrius set his book aside and let his thoughts drift.

Demetrius's mind meandered from the stories he'd heard about Ike Karas to Billy Williamson's request for help, then from specific memories of living in the Parish House to the comfort he took from the stability and feeling of permanence that Tolland offered. His struggles with his career careened into his thoughts, fighting against the calm Tolland instilled. When he'd left the law to write, the publishing world had been harsh and insular, but it made room—not much room, but some—for newcomers. By the time Demetrius's first book appeared, the growth of self-publishing was beginning. Before he'd finished his third, it had become an avalanche. In a matter of a year or two, millions of books became available. Even books meriting praise got lost in the tsunami, and while Demetrius wrote for the joy of it, the meager sales he generated were discouraging. He wasn't happy with the state of things, and it made writing well—no mean feat in the best of times—more challenging. And less satisfying.

All that came before Demetrius found himself in the clutches of Hollywood, an experience that crashed into his thoughts so forcefully that he stood and walked around the yard to banish it. Strolling and seeking less unsettling thoughts, he returned to Billy Williamson's plea for help. It seemed absurd to Demetrius that anyone would consider him competent to assist in a murder investigation; he had no training, and his experience was, literally, fictitious. And yet, he had absorbed what he'd heard from the Council members, Throop, and Wells with the practiced eye of one who created characters involved in crime.

Karas's arrogant and disquieting behavior made him an ideal victim, Clarke realized. And those Ike had trampled were equally intriguing suspects. A body on a chaise lounge discovered by a kid, a rookie cop thrust into circumstances well above his knowledge or experience, a quiet village roiled by a suspicious death—for Demetrius, this was milk and honey. But it was entirely possible, indeed quite likely, that Ike Karas had died absent mayhem or malicious intent. A heart attack, an undiagnosed illness, a fatal cocktail of self-medications—these seemed perfectly logical options.

Demetrius was certain he didn't want any part of a murder investigation in a town he cherished precisely because it was so serene, so comforting, and so gentle. He was just as certain that it would be a fascinating exercise to participate in an investigation that was, even this early, intriguing and compelling. So fraught that he found himself in a state of hopeless confusion, Demetrius turned to his only sure salvation. He went into the Inn, grabbed the Sunday Times magazine, and returned to his lawn chair to concentrate on the crossword puzzle.

Chapter 6

"CYANIDE."

"You're kidding."

"No sir," Billy Williamson said. "Ike Karas was poisoned. The pathologist says there's no doubt at all."

Demetrius felt the young officer's tension and noticed that his left foot was bouncing incessantly on the porch floor. "How?" he asked.

Billy had his notepad open on his lap, but he looked at Demetrius rather than at his notes. "How, what?"

"Injection? Something he ate or drank? One dose? Over time?"

Billy looked dejected. "We don't know. Well, *I* don't know. All I have so far is a call from the lab. They've done a preliminary exam. Haven't done all the lab work yet, and the guy says it'll be a while; no paperwork 'til then. Right before Karas bought it, a man over in Stafford Springs went bananas, killed his parents and two neighbors. Then, he turned himself in, quiet as a mouse. No idea what set him off, never mind why he took out the two folks next door. He was armed to the teeth. The lab guy told me Shultz—again, he's my boss—is all over everybody, including ballistics, medical examiners, and investigators, throwing his weight around to get the whole thing sorted out. It's a pretty big deal. Plus, the media's been all over it. So, Shultz wants it wrapped up yesterday."

"So Karas isn't a priority."

"Exactly. They tell me they'll get around to it, but . . . You don't know Shultz, but trust me, they want no part of pissing him off."

"So, it's down to you?"

"Yup. And you, I hope."

"We'll see about that. Do you have anything else? I saw you headed for the backyard over the weekend. You find anything?"

"Nothing new. There was a cup of coffee and a muffin on the table next to the body that morning. The crime scene guys took that stuff, and I didn't notice anything special on Saturday. The house is locked up, so I couldn't get in, but I've got a call in to Bonnie. That's Bonnie—"

"Bondurant, the real estate lady. You think she may have keys?"

"I'm hoping so. It's been a while since he bought the place, but she handled it, so maybe she held onto her set."

"Have you contacted the people who sold it?"

"No, why? Oh, maybe they still have their old keys?"

Demetrius nodded. "Or better still, they kept a spare key under the welcome mat or somewhere handy, forgot about it when they moved."

Billy jotted a note. "I hadn't thought of that," he said. "See? That's why I really need your help."

Demetrius took a deep breath. "Again, we'll see. All I'm willing to do right now is keep my promise. I said I'd talk with you about it."

"I really appreciate that."

"Do you have anything else? Who found the body?"

"The paperboy, Jimmy Dalton. Just a kid. I talked with him right after he found Karas. Karas made him deliver the paper to

45

the back deck. Kid said Ike sat out there every morning, in spring and summer. Couldn't be bothered to go to the front door for the paper, I guess."

"Did the kid notice anything when he found the body?"

"He remembered the coffee and the muffin but nothing else. Soon as he realized Karas was dead, he hot-footed it next door and had the neighbors call the cops."

"That was last Thursday morning, right?"

"Right."

"Have you talked to him again?"

Billy shook his head. "Nope."

"Planning to?"

"Well, sure. I called the house. His old man, Dennis, picked up. When I told him what I was after, he wouldn't call Jimmy to the phone. Said the kid's spooked. But when I talked to Jimmy that morning, he was cool."

Demetrius tilted his head back and gazed at the sky for a moment. "Kid's what . . . ten, eleven?"

"Thirteen."

"When I was that age, if I'd found a dead man, I would have been fascinated. I sure would have told everybody I knew about it. Pretty exciting stuff for a youngster, right?"

"Maybe. Or maybe it scared the pee out of him. First time I saw a horror movie, I didn't sleep for a week."

Demetrius grinned. "But it was like a car wreck, or maybe your first copy of *Playboy*, right? Couldn't get it out of your mind, couldn't stop talking about it, or at least thinking about it."

"Yeah."

"So, maybe his dad's just being overprotective."

"Whatever, but he still wouldn't put the kid on the phone." Williamson looked at his notepad. "He did say something I found kinda odd," he said. "I wrote it down, more or less. The old man said, 'who cares who killed that a-hole, anyway?'"

"I'm not sure it's that odd. I've already heard something similar from two other people."

Billy straightened up and looked directly into his companion's eyes. "You have? You've been asking around about this? You're already investigating." He didn't hide his enthusiasm.

Demetrius shrugged. "No big deal. I've been wandering about the village, drinking it all in, and this death—*murder* now—is on people's minds. I ran across a couple of the Town Council members, and they both said something to the effect that Karas deserved what he got."

"Who? Do they know something—maybe give us a lead?"

Demetrius laughed. "Slow down, cowboy. It was only gossip, just idle chitchat."

"That's no help," Billy said.

"It might get worse."

"How so?"

"Look, I've only been here for a weekend, so don't take this as gospel, but . . . There are at least three people in town who don't seem to care who killed Karas. If the guy was as unpleasant as everybody says—"

"General feeling in town is that he was a first-class prick."

"That's my point. If everybody thinks he got what he deserved, then maybe nobody cares who did it. Or worse, they know who did it, but they don't want the killer exposed or punished 'cause they think poisoning Karas was a, what, public service?"

"That's pretty ugly. I'd like to think Tolland is better than that."

"Me, too. But that won't make it so, Billy. If the consensus is that the town's better off without Ike Karas, people may be less than eager to help you find out who took him down. Maybe they'll even be inclined to protect the killer."

"That'll make my job much harder," Williamson said, frowning. "Just what I need."

"I could be wrong."

"Man, I hope so." The officer's phone buzzed and vibrated, and he checked the screen. "Gotta take this," he said. "Officer Williamson. How may I help you?" He listened, his eyebrows went up, and a modest smile appeared. "Yes, ma'am," he said. "I'll swing by within the hour. Yes, ma'am, sooner if I can." He disconnected and turned to Demetrius. "That was a housewife over on the other side of the pond. Says the neighborhood kids were playing ball in the street, somebody smacked a foul ball and broke one of her windshield wipers."

"Dear, dear," Demetrius said. "A suburban crime wave!"

"Right up there with murder by poison," Billy added, grinning. "No doubt about it. Still, I'm not nuts about ballgames in the street—kids paying zero attention to traffic. So, I'll go on over there and see if they can't move the game to someplace safer."

"Okay. Listen, I'm booked in this place for two more days. Anything else pops up, come on by, and we'll chat."

"I appreciate that," Billy said. "More than you know." He rose, put on his hat, and went down the porch steps two at a time. He was opening his car door when Demetrius came down the stairs to the sidewalk.

"Billy?"

"Yeah?"

"When I was Jimmy Dalton's age, you know where I was all summer long?"

"Nope."

"Crandell's Pond. Every kid in town was there. Every day."

Williamson thought for a moment. "Sooo . . . Jimmy Dalton?"

"*Exactly*. Odds are, he'll be there. If he isn't, all the other kids will be, and I'm betting he's told them all about his 'brush with death.'"

"Gotcha," Billy said, nodding enthusiastically.

When Demetrius went back into the Inn, Katherine Conrad came racing down the stairs, her apron flying and a damp mop in her hand. "You have a message, Mr. Clarke. I jotted it down on the pad next to the phone, over there on the check-in desk. You can read it, but it's from Bonnie. She says she's talked to the family that lives in Parish House, and you should give her a call."

"Thanks." Demetrius went to the desk and found the pink message slip. He folded it and slipped it into a pants pocket.

"You're welcome. It's unusual for guests to get messages here, you know? Everybody has their own phone now, right there in their pocket or purse, so taking messages doesn't happen very often. No need to leave a message with us when you can call the guests directly, you know? Good thing I had that pad handy, I guess." Katherine smiled. "All part of the service here at Tolland Inn!"

"Yes, very nice. Thanks again."

Demetrius settled into the chair in his room and dialed the number Katherine had carefully written out.

"Bonnie Bondurant."

"Hello, Ms. Bondurant. It's Demetrius Clarke, returning your call."

"Oh, yes, thanks for getting back to me. I ran into Meryl and Janice Young on Sunday. They're the folks who live in Parish House, and I told them about you and your history with their house and all."

"I see," Demetrius said. "Did you ask about a visit?"

"I didn't have to," Bonnie said, chuckling. "They're delighted that you're connected to their home, and they'd love to hear about what it was like in the old days. They'd like you to join them for dinner while you're here. Asked me to extend the invitation and give you their number."

"No kidding? That's terrific. And generous. I'd love to. Let me get a pen, and I'll take the number." Demetrius wrote their contact information down and thanked Bondurant heartily. He waited a few moments, reflecting on the New England warmth and the neighborliness that the Youngs' invitation embodied. Then, he dialed the number and arranged to visit Parish House that evening.

Demetrius walked down the hill to the convenience store, got his lunch, and took it and his book to the backyard. He spent the afternoon with his book, a turkey and Swiss cheese sandwich, and a sense of well-being and calm that felt almost alien to him.

Chapter 7

THE DAYLIGHT-SAVING SUN was beginning to fade when Demetrius tapped on the door to Parish House. The air was still, and the early evening was quiet but for an occasional car on the two roads that framed the property.

Janice Young opened the door. A little girl was standing just behind her, peeking around her mom's legs with wide eyes.

"Good evening. I'm Demetrius Clarke."

"Welcome! I'm Janice Young, and this is Abby." The little girl giggled and wrapped her arms around her mother's leg. "Meryl is just finishing some work for his PoliSci classes. He'll be with us in a moment. Abby, say hello to Mr. Clarke." Abby lowered her eyes and shook her head firmly. "Now, Abby, don't be shy. He's a nice man. He'll be having dinner with us." Abby tightened her grip.

"It's okay," Demetrius said, squatting down to make eye contact with the little girl. "I'm shy around people I don't know, too. We'll be shy together, okay?"

Abby nodded just a little.

Janice pulled the door fully open and ushered Demetrius into the entry hall. It was a little less dark with the door open wide, but it still felt cavernous to him. He followed as Janice, with Abby still firmly attached to her leg, led him down the hall and into the dining room. "Welcome back to Parish

House," Janice said.

A sense of comfort embraced Demetrius. There was the large dining room, the doors to side rooms and the kitchen, the windows beyond the dinner table facing a small enclosed porch, the narrow twisting staircase at the far end of the room, and the tiny room across from the staircase that had been Aunt Beth's studio. Everything was exactly as Demetrius remembered it. He drew an audible deep breath.

"Something wrong?" Janice inquired.

"No, no. On the contrary, it's perfect. Although, I'm not used to hearing 'Parish House.' We never called it that. The folks in town called it 'Church house' when I was here, which is my mom's family name. I didn't know about Parish until I got here last week."

Meryl Young emerged from the little room where Aunt Beth had bent over a drafting table to create precise pen and ink drawings. He introduced himself and welcomed Demetrius graciously. "Parish was an insurance guy," Meryl said. "As we understand it, he sold policies out of this room when he was growing the business. I don't know how this region came to be an insurance center, but there's no doubt that Hartford is home to dozens of insurance companies. Tolland had just this one, as far as I know. And this property was a farm as well, of course. How about some wine and the full tour?"

"We thought we'd do the backyard and the rest of the property outside first, before it gets too dark," Janice said, smiling.

"That would be delightful," Demetrius agreed.

They all went into the kitchen. Meryl opened and poured wine and filled a sippy-cup with juice for Abby. Demetrius walked over to the pantry just off the kitchen. Its configuration had not changed, but the shelves were new, and there was a rug covering the planked floor.

"We'll go out the back door," Janice said. "Abby, can you show Mr. Clarke what's on the back porch?"

Abby nodded and smiled, releasing her grip on her mother's leg, only to take her hand. "You come with us, mommy," she said.

The kitchen porch was large enough to accommodate a large box of toys, a scooter, a metal pedal car painted as a fire engine, a stroller, and a small sled. Abby went to the box, dug around, and came away with a stuffed creature. "This is Kanga," she said. "She likes to play in the yard."

"Kanga and I are old friends," Demetrius said. "I was very fond of her and Roo when I was your age."

They went down the stairs and entered the large yard. In front of them, a sizable garden bordered by several trellises displayed flowering plants in the earth and in pots and a large rectangle that held a well-maintained collection of rose bushes. Rose bushes climbed the trellises as well. Demetrius stopped at the edge of the garden and gaped, his eyes darting.

"Are you okay?" Janice asked.

"Yes. Just . . . strong memories. When my grandmother was well, before the years took their toll, she was in this garden every day. She wore a huge floppy sun hat and an apron and gloves, and she'd spend hours here, pruning, weeding, and tending. Sometimes, I could hear her humming. I often thought she was in a sort of trance."

"That sounds lovely," Janice said.

"I didn't understand, of course. I was devoted to running around and swimming and climbing trees, riding my bike all over town. As far as I was concerned, puttering with flowers was dumb. But she loved it, and her rose bushes were her pride and joy. They were right here," Demetrius said, gesturing at the rose bed, "just like this. I'm wondering, is it possible that—"

Janice reached out and took Demetrius's arm. "All these roses were here when we moved in," she said. "And the young couple who were here before us said they were here when they moved in, too. You're wondering if some of these roses are your grandmother's. I can't say for sure, but it's certainly possible."

Demetrius nodded and continued staring at the flowers until Meryl spoke. "The shed, over there behind the trees, still stands. And there's no doubt it was here when you were. Looking at it, it's hard to figure out how it's still upright, with beams and posts older than dirt. This place was built decades before the colonists humiliated the Red Coats, after all. The walls are made of planks, which I suspect weren't suitable for flooring. Come on, let's go have a look."

An earthen path led through a stand of birch trees to another swatch of green, narrower than the main backyard. On their left, the yard ended at the edge of Merrow Road. The shed stood along one side of the narrow yard. Demetrius walked into it, absorbing the rich aroma of its dirt floor and ancient, weather-beaten wooden walls. There were tools spread out on a worktable, and a couple of shovels, a rake, and a hoe leaned against the wall. The shelving above the tool table held a variety of gardening supplies, fertilizer and insecticides, and a collection of pots. A lawn mower and a snow blower were parked on a tarp, and three bicycles leaned against the aged and weathered wall at one end.

"I stored my bike here, too," Demetrius said. "I bet that one is yours, Abby. Am I right?"

She nodded. "Wanna see me ride?"

"Sure," Demetrius said.

The bike had training wheels, and the grass in the yard was

thick. So, Abby rode very slowly. But ride she did, streamers gently waving from the handlebars. Demetrius came out from under the shed and watched her, then turned left and walked a few steps to the edge of the shed to an area overgrown with shrubs and trees and weeds.

"When I was about Abby's age," Demetrius said, "there was a chicken coop back here. I can't remember how many, but we always had fresh eggs, and sometimes, for Sunday dinner, we'd have roasted chicken. I guess it got to be too much for Beth to manage, but one year, when I was a little older, it was gone." He looked back at the shed and smiled, turned, and took a narrow path back toward the large yard behind the rose garden. Meryl joined him. Janice helped Abby stow her bike, and then they followed along.

At the edge of the large yard, Demetrius stopped and pointed. "There was an asparagus patch here," he said, looking to his left. Then, turning to his right, "We had a badminton net set up right in the center of the yard."

"It's certainly big enough for that," Meryl noted. "I think it's possible that a full-sized tennis court could fit in this yard. It's certainly level enough."

A group of enormous trees bordered the lawn—a buffer between the yard and Cider Mill Road. When Abby and Janice caught up, Demetrius squatted down, pointed, and said to Abby, "I used to climb that tree, the tallest one right at the edge of the grass. I could go almost all the way to the top."

Abby looked up to the top of the tree. "That's very tall," she said.

"It certainly is," Janice agreed. "Too tall for little girls."

"Maybe when you're older," Meryl suggested. His wife shot him a look. "Or maybe not."

"I think our meal must be close to ready," Janice said.

"Let's go back in. Abby, you'll need to wash up for supper, okay?"

"Okay."

"Supper," Demetrius repeated. "One of my favorite words. Very New England. You don't hear folks in LA talk about having 'supper.'"

Meryl chuckled. "Probably don't hear 'em talking about Yankee pot roast, either," he said, "but that's what Janice is serving. Let's go on in. I see your wine glass is empty, and we can't have that."

Meryl and Demetrius helped Janice carry serving dishes from the kitchen to the table. Abby came into the room and marched up to her father. "See?" She held out her hands, turning them over for inspection.

"Clean as a whistle, Abs," Janice noted. "Excellent."

Abby beamed.

"Demetrius, take that chair if you would," Janice said. "I don't think you'd fit in the one with Abby's booster in it."

Demetrius nodded and walked around the table. As he did, several of the floorboards creaked under his feet, and he laughed. Meryl cocked his head and raised his eyebrows. "I know that sound as well as I know my name," Demetrius said, smiling broadly. "A couple of centuries and more, but the place hasn't changed much at all."

They sat and passed serving dishes around. Then, Meryl raised his glass. "To Parish House," he said, "proof positive that age doesn't necessarily come before beauty." They toasted, then Meryl continued. "I have great admiration for the folks who actually farmed this land. It's not exactly conducive to crops. The stone fence near the front door runs down to the end of our land, along Cider Mill. It's long, and I bet every single stone in that fence came from this property. Can you imagine the grit it took to clear that many rocks and haul them out just to plant vegetables?"

"That fence is absolutely straight and level, one end to the other," Janice said. "Marvelous craftsmanship. Do you suppose it ever occurred to them, in 1730, that their work would still be here? It does make one think."

"Sure does," Meryl agreed. "It makes me think they left no stone unturned."

Demetrius laughed at the pun. Janice groaned.

"So, are you enjoying your stay here?" Meryl asked.

"I am," Demetrius replied. "It's just as pleasant and as peaceful as I recall it."

"If you don't count murder," Janice said.

"What on earth are you talking about?" Meryl asked.

"Well, I would have told you when you got home, dear, but you went straight into your office before I had the chance. That man Karas, up on the Green—the one who died last week—it turns out he was poisoned. The news is all over town."

"You're kidding."

"No, she's not," Demetrius confirmed. "I talked with the local cop this morning. Mr. Karas was killed with cyanide."

"I'll be damned," Meryl exclaimed.

"Language, please, dear," Janice said, nodding to Abby. "But since it was Karas, 'damned' *is* rather appropriate, don't you think?"

Demetrius looked toward her. "Did you know him?"

"Indirectly," Janice replied. "Several years ago—this was just before Meryl and I got married—we lived in Manhattan. Meryl was working on his doctorate, but I had a job with a tiny little company. The staff members were mostly programmers. They called themselves the Bum Squad, working on programs for PCs. They were dreaming up apps and writing code, and they were good at it—creative and clever—but they couldn't speak English."

Meryl said, "Well, they could; it just wasn't the English the rest of us speak. That's where Janice came in."

Janice continued: "When you asked any of them about their work, they'd go into what I called digi-speak: technical jargon only they could understand. They couldn't translate their work into language average people could grasp, so they hired a marketing department. I was the department."

"They hit pay-dirt," Meryl said. "They developed a program that made household bookkeeping as easy as sending an email. HoManager."

"I've heard of that," Demetrius said.

"Everybody has by now," Janice said. "Back then, we were barely able to get things done. But word got out, and suddenly, we had venture capital people sniffing around. The Bum Squad called them 'Vulture Capitalists,' but we all realized we needed help, and a sizable investment, to go from start-up to mainstream."

"Enter Ike Karas," Meryl said.

"Yes. He pitched our founders hard. He promised the moon, kept leaning on them, and dangled huge money in front of them. There were others, but Karas kept upping the ante, and finally, they couldn't resist. They sold him a controlling share of the company and got real rich real fast."

"Sounds like a good deal for everybody," Demetrius said.

"It was . . . for about six months."

"What happened?"

"Ike Karas fired everybody except two programmers and then took it public," Janice answered. "He brought in some people from San Jose. Most of us, including me, ended up on the sidewalk."

"Literally on the sidewalk," Meryl added. "Day before he went public, Karas comes to their shop and sits everybody down. He said exactly three words to them: 'Get out now.' Then, a gang of security guards appeared and muscled everybody out. Didn't even let anybody clean out their desks."

"I'm still doing what I did then, just not for Karas. He hired an agency to manage their communications. Now, I freelance. It works for us because I can do most of it remotely, so it turned out okay."

"Except, you should have had shares," Meryl said. "We could be almost as rich as those two bozos who sold the place out from under you."

"It must have been awkward when he moved to Tolland," Demetrius suggested.

"Not for us," Meryl replied. "The one and only time we saw him was when he deigned to visit the swap meet, exactly once, and we were there. He didn't have any idea who Janice was, and he ignored us. It wasn't personal since he ignored everybody 'round here unless he had some reason to insult them."

"Just as well," Janice said. "My Meryl is a reasonable, calm fellow, but when he heard Karas had moved to Tolland, he was ready to beat him up."

"Not true," Meryl objected. "I believe what I said was, 'Somebody ought to knee-cap that bas—"

Janice threw one hand up. "Not in front of you-know-who," she cautioned.

"Right. Suffice it to say, I thought the guy deserved a whole lot less than that grand old house he bought. But he never paid the price for being an SOB. Well, not until now, that is. Cyanide, eh? Just desserts. Speaking of which, do we have any?"

"Any what, dear?"

"Dessert, of course."

After dinner, the two men bussed the table while Janice took Abby upstairs to get ready for bed. Meryl topped off their wine glasses and invited Demetrius to join him to say good-night to Abby.

The staircase was narrow, and the treads were small and tightly packed, and both men climbed hard against the wall where the treads were widest. The stairs made a complete U-turn, ending on a small landing, perhaps a yard square. To the right, one step up from the landing, was the door to Abby's room—the one where Demetrius had slept. They went in and found Janice tucking Abby in.

"Have a good sleep," Demetrius said to Abby, extending his hand. "It was a pleasure to meet you. Please tell Kanga that I was happy to visit with her, too."

Abby shook Demetrius's hand. She was on the verge of sleep, but she smiled brightly. Her parents each gave her a kiss. Abby switched off the light by the bed, and the three adults left the room.

At the landing, a second step led down the hall to the master bedroom. Demetrius automatically stretched his gait and bypassed the landing to step into the hall. "Sense memory," he whispered. "I always skipped that step on my way to the bathroom."

Meryl led them down the hallway, past the bathroom, and into the larger master bedroom. Its windows looked out over the garden and the large yard, now dark. Janis switched on a light. "I wanted you to see this," she said, gesturing to the wall opposite the bed.

The wall was decorated with family pictures: Meryl and Janice at their wedding, the wedding party, shots of the couple on vacations, several photos—posed and candid—of the three Youngs. In the center of the display was a simple black frame. When Janis pointed it out, Demetrius walked over to be closer to it. It was a precise, simple, elegant drawing of Parish House, viewed from the top of the vee formed by Cider Mill and Merrow Roads. "That's Aunt Beth's," Demetrius said.

"Yes," Janice confirmed. "This was downstairs when we moved in. The previous owners left it behind. We thought it belonged up here with our other pictures. After all, this house is the center of our life now."

Demetrius stared at the drawing for several minutes before he turned back to his hosts. "Thank you," he said. "I cannot express to you how much this visit means to me." His tone was quiet, and his eyes were damp.

Chapter 8

"THE BRADFORDS THINK they left a front door key to their old house under a flowerpot on the front stoop," Billy Williamson revealed. "I'm going to have a look inside Karas's house. Care to come along?"

"Not especially." Demetrius was nursing a cup of coffee in the living room at the Inn.

"Why not?"

"I'm leaving today," Demetrius reminded him. "I need to pack and settle up with the Conrads, and I'm supposed to be at Bradley by 2, 2:30 at the latest."

"We'll go now," Billy suggested. "You'll be back here in plenty of time."

"Hardly the point," Demetrius replied.

"Sorry?"

"Look, Officer—"

"Billy. Please."

"Billy, then. This was supposed to be a mini-vacation, just a quick visit. If I go with you, if we find something interesting, what good will it do? I'm gone before nightfall."

Billy nodded, his eyes on the floor. "You're sure? It would be great, and it would make me feel a whole lot better to have somebody I can work with who knows what's what. Somebody to lean on."

"I understand that, but, as I said, I'm scheduled to—"

"Hear me out. It never occurred to me that the Bradfords might have left a key behind. That was your suggestion. And it paid off, right? Mr. Clarke, it's a murder. Serious stuff, and my first time at the rodeo, you know? I've just started investigating, and I've already missed something you saw right off the bat."

"But you have a whole department behind you. Your boss, for one. And surely there are some major crime guys, professionals, you can consult?"

"Not a great idea."

"Why not? Isn't that why they're there?"

"Art Shultz, our commander, is a stickler for what he calls 'smart allocation.' He likes it when everybody stays in their lane, does their own job without wasting other people's time. When I have stuff that needs lab work, that's cool, it's their job. But if I spend half my time distracting detectives from their assignments, especially when all the senior guys are tied up with that quadruple killing in Stafford Springs, then—"

"Your boss'll get cranky. I understand that. But I don't have the expertise your force does, and while I'm not exactly overjoyed to be headed back to LA, it's where my home is, and I do have obligations there. It's time for me to get back to it."

"There's something else," Billy said.

"What?"

"I like this town, Mr. Clarke. It's a special place. I think you feel the same way."

"I have great affection for Tolland; it's true."

"So, it's okay with you if somebody gets away with murder here?"

"Of course not. But—"

"I'm afraid that's exactly what will happen if I'm on my own, Mr. Clarke. I don't think either one of us wants that. *I*

63

sure don't."

Demetrius met the officer's eyes and held them, appraising him until he broke out in a broad smile. "An appeal to my better nature, eh? You assume I have one, Billy, my friend."

"I'm pretty confident about that. I think you're probably a good guy, comes down to it. Besides, didn't you tell me you're kind of at loose ends right now? How did you describe it? I think you said you're 'floundering,' not all that happy with your work. Wouldn't a real investigation be a good distraction, maybe even put you back on track?"

Demetrius gave his companion another penetrating look. "I'll give you this, Billy: right behind that 'Aw, shucks, I'm just a raw rookie,' there's one pretty shrewd fellow."

Billy grinned. "I *am* a rookie," he said, "but I know how to pay attention."

Demetrius went to the table near the windows and picked up a slice of cornbread. He nibbled at it and gazed out the window. Katherine Conrad was in the yard, tending to a patch of pansies. She appeared to be having a good time. Demetrius's shoulders rose and fell, and he turned around to face the officer. "I'll go with you this morning," he said. "After that, we'll see."

"Great!"

"But I'm warning you now, if I scrub my flight, it's going to cost me. Not good for my budget. Not good at all . . ."

"But won't it be worth it if you can do something important for Tolland?"

"You really don't play fair," Demetrius said.

"All's fair," Billy replied. "Let's get going, shall we?"

The key was where the Bradford family had left it, and it turned the lock on the front door to Ike Karas's home easily. Billy went in first. "Tolland police!" he shouted. "Anybody here?" There was no response, so he pulled the door fully open and beckoned Demetrius in.

The front door fed a hallway that ran straight to the back of the house. At the end of the hall, on the left, a stairway led to the second floor. To the men's immediate left, a set of glass French doors led to a dining room.

The men walked into the dining room. It featured a long teak table with seating for eight. The walls were forest green, and the shades on the windows facing the street were drawn; at midday, the room was evening dark. Billy turned and found a switch on the wall and flipped it, igniting a dozen lights recessed into the ceiling. "Geez, that's bright!"

"And all wrong," Demetrius said.

"Huh?"

"Stand in the front yard, and there's no doubt this is a perfect mid-1700s house. But that lighting is contemporary. This room wants a chandelier and an antique sideboard, maybe a china cabinet with glass doors. Recessed halogens just don't fit."

"I see what you mean," Billy said. "They probably didn't use a lot of teak back then, and the table is, what, Danish? Still, you could do a pretty nifty dinner party in here."

"You could," Demetrius agreed. "But I don't think Karas did."

Billy looked around the room, frowning. "No?"

"No. There's nothing on the table. There's no centerpiece, no placemats, nothing. I don't see any evidence that it's ever been used. Let's see. Walk over to the chair at the head of the table and tilt it back a bit."

Billy did.

"See?"

"See what?"

"Look down. Those indentations in the carpet are deep. I don't think that chair has been moved since it was put in its place. Probably the same all the way around the table."

Billy reached down and stuck a finger in the indentation where the chair had rested. "I wouldn't have thought of that," he said.

There was a door in the dining room, opposite the street windows. Demetrius walked over and pushed it open. "Kitchen," he said. "It's all wrong, too."

Billy joined Demetrius in the doorway. They each absorbed what they saw: bright red appliances, a chrome and glass refrigerated wine cabinet, an island in the center of the room with an elaborate stove beneath a stainless-steel pot rack. In one corner, a red leather banquette framed a black lacquered table.

"At least he used this room," Billy noted, pointing. "There are some magazines and papers on that table."

"Yeah," Demetrius said. His brow was furrowed, and there was a hint of ire in his voice. "The more I see, the less I like this man."

"Now what?"

"This room belongs in a modern Manhattan condo. I get that's his style, if he had any—and I doubt that he did—but it's just out of place in this home. There's more. Look there." Demetrius pointed to the wall above the sinks. It held a red metal back splash that reached the ceiling.

"Nothing there but that red thing," Billy observed.

"Exactly. I got twenty bucks says there was a window right there to let some light in and give whoever lived here a sense of the outside world. I'll bet you he tore it out. Disgusting. Let's move on."

The men walked to the back of the kitchen. Demetrius paused when he noticed an expensive radio on the banquette table. He reached over and turned it on. "Talk radio," he said. "No surprise there."

"No?"

"Nope. As far as I can tell, there's nothing musical about this guy."

"Huh. That the sort of thing you writers think about?"

"Sure. A guy who listens to classical or opera is not the same as a guy who listens to jazz or Lady Gaga or oldies. This fellow listened to none of that. Tells us something about him."

"If you say so," Billy said.

Demetrius reached out and turned the radio off. A glint of light caught his eye, and he looked down. "What have we here?" he remarked.

"What?"

"Look." Demetrius pointed to the corner of the banquette where the top and bottom cushions met.

"Are those blueberry muffins?"

"In a plastic bag," Demetrius pointed out.

"Wow."

"Yeah. I don't need to tell you—"

"No, sir. I'm putting on gloves. I'll take pictures to show exactly where it was when we found it, and I'll write a tag and tape it on." Billy pulled out his notepad and his phone. "How many do you see?"

"Five."

Billy snapped off four photos. "Got it." He gently extracted the bag and laid it on the counter. "Let's move on."

The men went through two swinging doors into a pantry lined with sleek black shelves. At the end of the pantry was a closed door. Billy opened it. "Bingo," he said. "Ike's office."

The furniture was modern. There were two computers on a large desk, two filing cabinets against one wall, an ergonomic desk chair, and two leather director's chairs opposite the desk. "This'll keep you busy for a while," Demetrius said. "Personal papers, maybe a will, work materials, emails, social media connections. You'll learn a lot in here."

Billy pulled out his notepad and made rapid notes. "You meant '*we*,' right?" Billy asked. "*We'll* learn a lot."

Demetrius chuckled. "Persistence," he said. "Always a welcome asset in an investigator." He walked around the desk to a door leading to the entry hall and opened it. The staircase was just outside the door. "You wanna go up or see what's on the other side of this hallway?"

"Let's finish down here first," Billy suggested. The men went down the hall toward the front and slid the pocket doors open. "Geez," Billy remarked.

The men stood at one end of a great room that ran the length of the house. Large sofas and easy chairs sat near the street windows. In the middle, a massive leather sectional surrounded a long low coffee table facing a sizable fireplace. Beyond that, more couches and chairs faced the back of the room. The wall at the far end had been torn down and replaced with large sliding glass doors that looked out to the deck and the backyard.

"This is infuriating," Demetrius said. "This space was almost certainly three rooms before he gutted them." He pointed to the seating area near the front windows. "That would have been a parlor. There would have been a wall and doors so they could close off the parlor during the winter and stay warm in the sitting room with the fireplace. The room at the back would have been a summer room, looking out onto the property, but it would have been closed off from the sitting room, too. He destroyed it all." Demetrius's tone grew more aggrieved as he spoke.

"I'll give him this," Billy said, "he made it *his* place."

"Indeed, he did," Demetrius agreed. He did a long slow turn, taking in the entire space. "No sense of history, no respect for heritage, not a shred of decency. He didn't even appreciate the original flooring; he's carpeted every square inch of this place. It would be criminal to take up the original floors, but it wouldn't surprise me to find he did exactly that. Bastard."

"Wow. You're steamed."

Demetrius, his jaw tight and his eyes blazing, said, "I was in Parish House the other day, visiting the Young family. They, and everybody who lived there before them, exercised great care to preserve the beauty of that home. They cherish the past that lives in the house with them. But *this* moron? He trampled all over those values."

Billy was so startled by Demetrius's flaring fury that he said nothing for a couple of minutes. "Let's keep going," he finally urged.

The men left the great room and walked back down the hall to the staircase. One side of the stairs was a wall; on the other, a glistening chrome banister sloped its way from bottom to top. "You cannot be serious," Demetrius said.

"What, that chrome thing? It is pretty show-offy."

"A sin in its own right. He even carpeted the staircase. I hope he didn't take up the original treads."

"I heard something about that," Billy said.

"What?"

"Mr. Karas heard that Jeff does fine woodwork—whole town knows that—and asked him to take out the original staircase and build a new one."

"Let me guess," Demetrius said, "Jeff refused."

"In no uncertain terms."

"Good for him."

Upstairs, a hallway exactly like the one on the first floor separated two sides of the house. On one side, two smaller bedrooms were separated by a bathroom. On the other, Karas had created a master suite with an enormous bed, a leather recliner, a sizable walk-in closet, and a master bath with a jacuzzi. The suite was on the back side of the house, and Demetrius noted that Karas had replaced the original windows overlooking the backyard with modern ones. Toward the front of the house, beyond the master suite, Karas had established a recreation room. It had a huge wall-mounted television screen, a teak game table with an inlaid checkerboard and matching chairs, and another large sectional couch. On one wall, there was a carefully arranged group of basic black frames, each containing a business logo.

"Get out your phone and take pictures of these," Demetrius said. Billy did. "What do you see, Billy?"

"Looks like a bunch of ads," Billy said.

"Yes, but this is more than that. Have you seen any other artwork in this place?"

Billy paused, concentrating, then said, "Just those weird modern blotchy things in the great room."

"Right. So, what's missing?"

Billy looked confused. To cover the look, he took a moment to put his phone back in his pocket and, looking at it, he smiled. "Aha. Photos!"

"Exactly. No family portraits, no girlfriend or boyfriend, no colleagues. No diplomas or certificates in his office, no snapshots on the fridge. Nothing. This wall shows us the only thing he cared about."

"Business," Billy noted.

"Yes, unless I've totally misunderstood this man," Demetrius said, nodding. "I'll bet he's got ties to each of those companies. He owns them, or he's got a major stake in them, but they matter to him somehow. They appear to be the only thing that did. And the money they generated, of course. This place reeks of excessive wealth." Demetrius checked his watch. "I need to get back to the Inn," he said.

"I'll walk you back," Billy offered. "I'll come back here later and start sniffing around in his office."

The men went down to the front door and exited. Billy used the extra key to lock the door and leaned down to put it back under the flowerpot.

"Don't," Demetrius warned.

"Don't what?"

"Don't leave that key where anybody can find it."

Billy nodded. "Somebody might want to get in here and mess around with stuff."

"Exactly. You don't want that."

"Nope."

The men went down the sidewalk and turned toward the Inn. Tenny Baker was coming toward them, pushing her fancy walker.

"Uh-oh," Demetrius said.

"Problem?"

"Not exactly. A couple of days ago, I promised to stop in at her place for a visit. I'd forgotten about it."

"'Uh-oh' is right, then," Billy agreed.

"Why?"

"I may not be a seasoned detective, but I know this town," Billy said. "Anybody with good sense doesn't dare get sideways of Tenny Baker. She's a force to be reckoned with."

"Yeah," Demetrius agreed. "I'm going to need a good excuse."

Billy chuckled. "It probably won't help."

When the men met Tenny on the sidewalk, she greeted them with steely eyes. "I trust you have drawn a bead on the disreputable soul who killed Mr. Karas," she said, pointing at Billy. And then, leveling her glare at Demetrius, "And you, sir, owe me a visit. My apple cobbler is gone, but I'm headed home to bake a pie. When should I expect you?" Tenny and Billy both looked at Demetrius, who hesitated and shrugged. "Well?"

"Perhaps I can find time tomorrow," Demetrius said.

"I'll expect you around ten."

Billy caught Demetrius's eye and winked at him. "Another day in Tolland will be good for you," he said. "For me, too."

Chapter 9

JEFF AND KATHERINE CONRAD were sitting at a porce-
lain-topped table in the Inn's kitchen, both in handsome
wooden chairs. Katherine was wearing a smock. Jeff was in his
overalls and faded red tee shirt. Demetrius wondered if it was
the same shirt or Jeff had a drawer full of them.

"Hi," Katherine greeted Demetrius. "Would you like to
join us for lunch? I've made egg salad, and there's a fresh loaf
of rye here. That little dish has bacon crumbles in it. Jeff likes
to mix them into the egg salad. I don't. We've got plenty;
you're welcome to sit. Jeff, get Mr. Clarke a chair."

Jeff started to rise, but Demetrius waved him off. "No,
thanks," Demetrius said, smiling. "I had an extra slice or two of
your delicious corn bread this morning. I'm still quite full."

"Okay," Katherine said. "I believe you're leaving us today.
Flying home, right? I can check you out, but we need to go out
to the desk in the lobby to do that. Would you like to close out
your bill now?" She rose to come around the table.

"No need," Demetrius said. "Please sit. I'd like to extend
my stay for another day or so. I assume you have room for
me?"

"Of course," Katherine said. "You're our only guest right
now. No reservations until Thursday. We've got three booked
for the weekend. Would you like to stay where you are? You
can, of course. But now that the Daltons have left, that room is

available. It's larger, and it has a desk. The windows overlook the backyard, so it's pretty and very quiet. It's my personal favorite. Would you care to switch?"

"No, thank you. I'm content with the one I'm in, and I like the view of the Green."

"Okay," Katherine said. "I'm glad you like it. Do you know how long you're going to stay?"

"Not precisely. Another day, perhaps a few more."

Jeff looked up from his plate. "Offica Williamson?"

"That's one reason," Demetrius said.

Jeff turned to Katherine. "No cha'ge."

"I don't understand," Katherine said.

"No cha'ge for the room, long as he's he-ah."

"But—"

"No cha'ge!"

"Why?"

"Murder in Tolland. Won't do. This fella's helping. No cha'ge."

Katherine opened her mouth again, but Jeff, watching her, shook his head just once. Both Katherine and Demetrius understood. Jeff had said all he would.

"Well, there you have it," Katherine said. "Unless we get more bookings than we can handle, Tolland Inn is your home for now. Would it be okay with you if we let Lucinda change the bed linens every other day? She'll still make the room up, just as perfectly as she always does. But if she doesn't have to do laundry every day—"

"That's fine with me," Demetrius answered. He moved closer and stood near Jeff. "You are gracious and generous, Mr. Conrad. You and Katherine are what Tenny Baker calls 'good Tolland people.' I am most grateful."

Jeff nodded once and returned to his sandwich.

* * *

By 2:30 that afternoon, Billy Williamson had patrolled roughly half of Tolland, warned some kids riding their bikes near the school to ride with traffic, not against it, and written a report on a fender bender at the entrance to the parking area at Crandell's Pond. He also arranged to have the lab pick up the plastic bag containing muffins from Ike Karas's kitchen. Lieutenant Shultz was not in his office, and Billy gladly departed before his commander returned.

Billy bought a packaged breakfast sandwich at the convenience store and drove to Ike Karas's house. He let himself in and went down the hall to the office, where he opened his notepad, took a sizable bite of his lunch, and pulled open the top drawer of one of the filing cabinets. The files contained business materials, contracts, agreements, tax documents, and dozens of bureaucratic forms.

Billy found it tedious but perused every file, just in case. Several of the files contained documents on works-in-process and included correspondence. Billy found several angry exchanges, including Karas berating colleagues for their ineptitude and insulting a contractor for shoddy work and two others for overcharging. The top three drawers of the second filing cabinet bore testimony to Karas's approach—all three were stuffed with litigation documents. It took some time, but Williamson determined that most of the cases, including several wrongful termination cases, had been settled. When courts had ruled, Karas lost more often than he won.

In the desk, there was a drawer for files, where Williamson found materials more closely tied to Tolland. The drawer contained several documents pertaining to Karas's efforts to raze his house and at least as many concerning his efforts to unseat members of the Town Council.

Another batch of files delineated invoices for all the work that had been undertaken after Karas purchased the house. By Williamson's rough calculations, Karas had spent nearly as much renovating the house as he had to purchase it, a fact which caused Billy to pause and ponder the result of the man's lavish spending. *All that money*, he thought, *spent on a house nobody else would want to live in, or, if Demetrius was right about the dining room, even visit.*

Billy hit the switch to fire up the computer, and a screen appeared asking for a password. He thought about logical choices: birth date, initials, the street address of the house. But he hesitated to try them for fear he'd fail too often and lock himself out. He sat in frustration for several minutes before he pulled his phone out and dialed a number.

"Hello," a voice answered.

"Mr. Clarke, this is Billy."

"Yes?"

"I need your help." Billy explained his dilemma. "Any ideas?"

"I don't recall. Is there a blotter on the desk?"

"Yes,"

"Lift it up and look under it."

Williamson did. "Nothing," he said.

"Check the center drawer in the desk. Probably looking for a Post-it."

Williamson did. "Nope."

"Somewhere on the computer or the monitor?"

"All clear."

"Hmmm. Okay, what else is on the desk?"

"There's a stapler, a stamp dispenser, a fancy calculator, a mug with pens in it, a lamp with a green shade, matching scissors and letter opener, and a couple of pads of paper."

"Look at the bottom of the mug."

Billy picked it up and held it high enough to examine its bottom.

"There's one of those Post-it thingies on the bottom. It says IK12345."

"How original," Demetrius said. "Try it."

There was a pause, and then Billy said, "Bingo!"

"Good luck."

"Thanks."

Demetrius spent the afternoon in his room on the phone and his laptop. He postponed his return flight and agreed to the extra fees that change triggered, noting with sarcasm that he had no choice. He checked in with a neighbor near his small house in LA's Wilshire District to make sure all was well there. It was. He contacted the post office to extend his vacation hold on mail. It took three transfers and a seventeen-minute wait to extend the hold on his *LA Times* subscription. He went through his emails, responding to a request relayed by his publisher to join a panel discussion of mystery writers in Burbank. He ignored several notes from a TV producer he knew but did not care to engage. He checked his bank accounts and paid a couple of utility bills online. He called the rental car agency to tell them he was keeping their car for a few more days.

When finished tying up loose ends, Demetrius pulled a book of crossword puzzles from his briefcase and spent some time solving one. He showered and went downstairs, telling Katherine he'd be out for the evening to free her from the need to set out wine and snacks. He took his rental car on the slow, sylvan road to Rockville and strolled its historic district before he found a restaurant that had a bar. He had a drink before he moved to the dining room for dinner.

Back in Tolland, Demetrius parked the car and walked the entire length of the Green, up past the intersection just outside the Inn and down to the old Town Hall. The air was pleasant, and the town was serenely quiet. A few homes were dark, but most were lit, and in many, he could see the flickering frenetic flashes of light and color from TV sets. It occurred to him that there was not a television in his room at the Inn and that he had not missed it at all.

Demetrius noted that the Karas house was dark except for a porch light, a light on the driveway, and, glowing at the back of the house, some lights on the deck. He assumed they all operated on timers. A few doors beyond, there were lights on in Zoey Caldwell's cottage—the first signs of life there since Demetrius had arrived. Zoey had been the youngest resident on the Green during Rus-D's summers. She was a writer who had inherited the cottage when her parents died. Demetrius had no specific memories of her other than a vague sense that, as a starving artist, she'd seemed a romantic figure. He made a mental note to look her up on his laptop, curious to see how her career had progressed.

Demetrius reentered the Inn quietly, hoping to escape a prolonged conversation with Katherine. Then, he slipped into his room to read until he grew bleary enough to sleep.

* * *

The next morning, Demetrius brushed his teeth and shaved, threw on the last of his clean polo shirts and khakis, grabbed his driving cap, and walked down the Green. After he knocked on the door, he waited quietly until it opened. "Good morning, young man," Tenny greeted him. "You're a skoosh early, but I'm quite ready for you. Do come in."

Tenny led Demetrius to the kitchen, which overlooked her

backyard. There was a small table abutting the windows. The table was set for two with matching china cups and saucers, matching cream and sugar servers, brightly polished silverware, and a bouquet of pansies in a small antique cobalt blue vase. The kitchen was bright, its yellow walls cheery, and its aromas—coffee and baked goods—inviting.

"Sit there, please," Tenny requested. "I'll get everything ready."

"May I help?"

"No, thank you. Been here on my own for so long now that I know exactly where everything is, so it's easier to do for myself than give directions to somebody else. Took me a long time to train that girl Lucinda to put everything back where it belongs when she cleans for me."

"I imagine that's the same Lucinda who takes care of the Inn," Demetrius said. "She does a fine job there."

"Needed some training when she came to me," Tenny said. "So many young people have no sense of order or purpose these days. She's energetic, no doubt, and I give her credit for making her own way. I see so many youngsters lollygagging about, no direction. She's not one of them, bless her soul."

As she spoke, Tenny carried a small apple pie and a coffee carafe to the table. She went to a cabinet drawer and produced a pie slicer, returning to pour the coffee before she sat. Demetrius noticed that the fancy walker was behind her chair; she hadn't used it when she greeted him, and she navigated the kitchen without it.

"It just occurred to me . . ." Tenny said. "Would you prefer tea?"

"No, thank you."

Tenny nodded and took her seat across from Demetrius. "So, young man," she began, "I hear you're planning to buy

Parish House."

Demetrius was moving a spoonful of sugar toward his coffee cup, and he suspended the spoon in mid-air. "No," he said. "I'm not, even if Bonnie Bondurant is eager to have me do so. As near as I can tell, she's shared her hope with everyone in town. I did ask her to arrange for a visit, but that was only in pursuit of a trip back in time, not a purchase."

"You've met the Youngs, then?"

"I have. They were kind enough to have me over for supper. I liked them. Their daughter, Abby, is a charmer."

"He's at the University, over t'Storrs," Tenny said. "Never much cared for those people, rowdy youngsters and snooty professors. But he seems nice enough."

"He's a good host. He certainly appreciates his good fortune, living in that house. So does Janice."

"I hear she works," Tenny said, "like so many women these days who don't settle for being housewives."

Demetrius wasn't sure if she was approving or not.

"It all started with the vote, you know," Tenny continued. "Once that happened, it was only a matter of time until they wanted to work, run for office, all that. I don't regret much, but I'm sorry I missed out on all that. I was caught betwixt and between, you see. I was too early to join them, too late to change my ways once we'd settled down here."

"I remember you being very active here in town," Demetrius recalled. "You were always in charge of things. Wasn't that the same as women who had careers? You did a lot of work for Tolland."

Tenny snorted. "Huh. When you get paid, even if you get paid less than men, you earn a measure of respect. Zoey Caldwell, across the street, struggles to sell her work. But most 'round here respect her because she makes enough to keep going. I never earned a dime, so folks always thought I was just a do-gooder. Not the same thing at all."

"I'm sure your efforts were appreciated."

Tenny giggled. It was surprisingly youthful. "I wasn't the gentlest woman in town. I suspect that I was more feared than appreciated. But you're kind to say otherwise. Let's try that pie, shall we?" She pulled it over and raised the pie cutter, bringing it down with enough force that the table shivered just a little. She cut two wedges of precisely the same size and slid them onto plates.

Demetrius sliced his wedge with his fork and took a bite. "That's excellent," he said. "Just enough cinnamon, perfect crust. The apples are delicious, too. Are they local?"

Tenny finished chewing her first bite and then grinned. "You could say that," she said and pointed out the windows to a back corner of her yard.

Demetrius followed Tenny's direction and saw six mature apple trees evenly spaced to form a perfect square. There were a few apples on the ground beneath the trees and an impressive crop of shiny red ones on the branches.

"I used to pick them myself," Tenny said, "until I couldn't manage. I asked Jeff to build me a ladder, but he refused. I wasn't happy about that, but he was right. Woman of my age has no business climbing trees. I have a gardener who cares for my flower bed out front. So, I've trained him on when to prune the trees and how to pick the apples at just the right time. Those trees are a blessing. They keep me busy, that's for sure."

Tenny again pointed, this time to a counter behind Demetrius. When he swung around, he saw two large colanders and a picnic basket, all filled with apples. "That's a lot of baking," Demetrius noted.

"It's even more applesauce," Tenny said. "You should buy

stock in Mason jars. I imagine they'd be out of business without me."

"Do you sell it?"

"Heavens no. I walk them around to my neighbors on the Green, take them to meetings and church and the library. I give several to my gardener and the man who takes care of my car. Dr. Kraskin insists on picking up several jars, too. And, of course, I give several dozen to Katherine, over t'the Inn, so her guests can enjoy genuinely local fare. After all that, if I have any apples left, I commandeer somebody from the swap meet to put them on a table out there, and they disappear."

Demetrius took another bite of pie. "If your applesauce is as good as this, you could make a fortune."

Tenny snorted again. "And do what with it? I've got what I need: my house, my garden and my trees, my old Ford runs fine, and I host our bridge club every other week. Most days, I've got places to go, things to do. What do I need with a fortune? Would you like more coffee?"

"No, thank you."

"Well, then, let's get right to it, shall we?"

"I'm sorry, get right to—"

"Well, the murder, of course. Hasn't been a killing in this town in I don't know how long. Of course, now and then, somebody drinks too much and drives to their death. But . . . *murder*? Not in our town. I understand that you're giving young Billy a hand. So, tell me what you know."

Demetrius chuckled. "I sincerely doubt I know as much as you do," he said. "I wasn't going to bring it up, but since you have, I'd much rather hear what *you* think."

Tenny settled back in her chair and cradled her coffee cup between both hands. She shifted a little to look out the windows. "Mr. Karas didn't deserve to be killed," she said. "But it's hardly a surprise that he was. He was rude and belligerent and arrogant. I've never known anyone to be less sociable. That man trampled over a nice young couple because he coveted a house on the Green in a town where everybody is everybody else's friend, but he never made a friend. He moved to a perfectly pleasant village and behaved unpleasantly from the day he arrived. I suppose you've heard that he wanted to tear that magnificent house down?"

"Yes, I have."

"Absolutely marvelous example of its type, historic in every sense, and he didn't give a hoot. If he felt that way about the house, imagine how he felt about Tolland. He had his way, he'd probably plow the Green under and install a fast-food restaurant. Despicable man."

"You know he was poisoned?"

"That's what the town says."

"And you know everyone, I imagine. You certainly used to. Do you have suspects in mind, Mrs. Baker? Suspicions?"

"Rusty, do you imagine I would indulge in gossip of that sort?"

Demetrius laughed. "I'd be sorely disappointed if you didn't," he said. "Just between us, of course."

"And Billy."

"Well, yes. Billy, too."

"It's a long list, sad to say," Tenny said. "Mr. Karas treated our Town Council like dirt. That whole bunch of 'em wanted to be done with him, even the ones he didn't try to run out of office. And my gardener tells me he refused to pay several of the men who worked on his house. Some of them might have wanted him alive, hoping they'd get paid, but others may have just given up and sought a different sort of payment. He constantly complained about noise from the playground at the

83

school down the hill from his house, got into arguments with several teachers and the principal. I heard he once threatened some kids who cut through his backyard on their way home, so there might be an angry father or two on the list. Comes down to it, the list of people who *didn't* have a reason to do Karas harm is shorter than the ones who did. By a country mile."

Demetrius noted that Tenny hadn't mentioned the Youngs' animosity toward Karas but concluded that they fit into her roster of "the ones who did." "Let me ask a different question," Demetrius said. "If we were to create a list of people Billy Williamson should talk to, who would you put on it?"

Still focused on her yard, Tenny drew a deep breath and furrowed her brows. "Virginia Irving," she said.

"Who's she?"

"The *Vernon Journal Inquirer*, our local paper," Tenny said. "Virginia was a reporter in Concord, up t'New Hampshire, before she and Walter moved here. She covers Tolland for the paper. I imagine she'll be asking around. Her stories are always good; she talks to the right people, and she gets her facts right. They live in that house at the top of Cider Mill Road, used to be the Snyders' place. She's all over town all the time: Town Council meetings, social gatherings, fundraisers. I'd talk to her."

"I'll suggest it to Billy, point him in her direction."

"That won't do. You're a tad out of touch, being away so long and all, but the day Art Shultz lets Billy or anybody else in his operation talk to a reporter, the world will stop turning and the dead will rise. Art doesn't want anybody saying anything to anybody, never mind say it to the press. If you want to find out what Ginny knows, you'll have to talk to her yourself. Art can't stop that."

"Oh, no. I promised Billy I'd help him sort this out, but I

don't have any authority. I'm just a sounding board."

"How disappointing."

Demetrius frowned. "Why?"

"You've got a good head on your shoulders, young man. No surprise, since you come from good Tolland folk. Billy's eager enough, and he seems to like it here, but he's just a kid. If he's going to solve this crime—"

"He needs me," Demetrius finished. "Trust me; he's made that quite clear."

"Then help him." It wasn't a suggestion; it was a command.

"It may take him some time," Demetrius said, "but I'm pretty sure he'll sort it out."

"I'm not," Tenny said.

"Why?"

"The reason I suggested the reporter, Virginia Irving, is that she's accustomed to sharing what she knows. That's her job, after all. I'm not so sure anybody else is going to be all that cooperative."

"I don't understand."

"Most folks in this town—at least the decent, honest ones—think we're better off without that man," Tenny answered, stabbing a finger in the direction of Karas's house.

"Are you suggesting that people are willing to cover up for his killer?"

"Oh, I imagine they'll agree that murder is a step too far. But that doesn't mean they'll go out of their way to help Billy find out who did it."

"Seriously?"

"Lots of folks chattering away about it," Tenny said. "And they seem to agree that Karas's death is no great loss. I'm not saying they condone it, but there's a good chance that nobody 'round here is inclined to go out of their way to catch whoever killed him."

"What about you?"

Tenny smiled. "A murder in Tolland is a black mark, that's for sure. But I doubt I know anything that would be of use to Billy."

"You're right across the street from Karas's house," Demetrius pointed out. "Did you notice anything unusual the morning the paperboy—"

"Jimmy Dalton."

"Yes, Jimmy . . . the day Jimmy found the body."

"I did not," Tenny replied.

"If you had, would you tell Billy?"

Tenny smiled again. "Might," she said. "Might not."

Chapter 10

O N HIS WAY BACK to the Inn, Demetrius noticed a flyer posted on a board in front of the library announcing a Town Council public meeting to begin planning the annual Tolland budget. When he got to his room, he gave Billy Williamson a call. "Are you going to the meeting this evening—the Town Council budget thing?"

"I am," Billy said. "I usually go to their meetings. It's a good way to keep up with what folks are fretting about and to stay in touch with the Council. For this one, Art will want me to be there just to make sure they aren't going to fool around with their public safety funds."

"I thought I'd drop in too."

"Great. I get there early to chat, listen to complaints. I'll introduce you around."

Demetrius had anticipated the offer. "Let's not do that," he said.

"Why not?"

"I'm getting the sense that people aren't too keen for your investigation to succeed. If they think I'm working for you—or with you—they might be less cooperative."

Billy laughed. "Oh, they know. Strongest thing in this town is its grapevine. You can't underestimate Katherine's capacity to chatter, and Tenny Baker and Bonnie Bondurant are right behind her. Can't see how walking in with me makes a difference."

"I agree that it's subtle. But sometimes appearances are important. If I'm with you, there won't be any doubt. If I'm alone, maybe it'll be a little more open. Besides, I'm going mostly 'cause I hope Ginny Irving will be there. I've been led to believe that you can't—"

"She's so far out of bounds that I won't even nod to her. Art's been known to tear guys a new one if they give anything to the media without his say-so. How'd you know about that?"

"I had brunch with Tenny this morning."

"'Nuf said. See you there?"

"Yes," Demetrius confirmed.

"Cool."

"So, any new leads? And what did Karas's desk tell you?"

"I'll get the easy part out of the way first," Billy said. "It's hearsay, but I don't think Jimmy Dalton can give us anything we don't already know."

"I'm not surprised," Demetrius said. "Why is it hearsay?"

"He and his family are on vacation, spending a long week-end at Misquamicut."

"We did that once when I was a kid," Demetrius recalled. "It's a great beach."

"Never been. Point is, I couldn't get to Jimmy, so I went down to the pond and talked to his buddies. Turns out, he wouldn't shut up about Karas, but all he knows is that he delivered the paper, found the body, and scooted next door to get the cops. Told everybody more than once how weird it was, seeing a dead guy in his fancy pjs."

"He saw the coffee and the muffin on the table, right?"

"Yeah. Told somebody the muffin looked so good that he was tempted to swipe it but decided it might get him in trouble with us—the cops, I mean."

"Okay. What about Karas's office?"

"Gimme a sec'." Demetrius heard Billy flipping through pages in his notepad. "For starters, there's a good number of people Karas worked with who got into tussles with him. I went through all that. A lot of them are far away. He did a lot of work with people in Seattle and San Jose, a big collection agency in Iowa, a couple of tech firms in Florida. Nothing to suggest any of them ever came to Tolland, though, so I figure they're off the list."

"Unless they arranged for *somebody else* to kill him," Demetrius suggested.

"Oh, sure, 'cause everybody knows that hit men use baked goods and French Roast coffee as weapons of choice."

"Good point. What else?"

"The folks he sued, or they sued him. But he either lost or settled with them, so they don't have much of a motive."

"Unless the settlement was miserly. Still, it's down to locals, right?"

"Yeah. Town Council, a handful of frustrated contractors, a couple of whom wrote him some nasty emails. He sure had some unpleasant things to say to the history buffs in town. He made an email file called Historical Hystericals. They all sent him letters about the importance of preservation. His answers were really nasty. But once the Town Council shot him down, all that stopped."

"And the house still stands," Demetrius said, "so they don't have an active beef with him."

Billy laughed. "Unless they've seen what he did inside. I know at least one fellow who's really hacked off about that."

Demetrius flinched. "Yes, about that . . . I regret that you had to see my anger. I thought about it later, and it seemed, what? Disproportionate, I guess. Kind of embarrassing. I apologize."

"It did seem a bit over the top," Billy agreed. "I thought about it later, too. I don't want to step where I don't belong."

"About that? It's over. I do apologize, though."

"No need," Billy reassured. "Only, I wondered if that's what you're really steamed about. I mean, what Ike did to that place is weird and disrespectful, no doubt about that. But you were so angry that, well, it just seemed kind of wacky, you know?"

"And?"

"Like I say, I don't want to mess around where I don't belong, but the first time we talked, you said you'd been in . . . gimme a second, I want to get this right. You said you'd just escaped from an ugly corner of hell."

Demetrius held his phone away from his ear and stared at it before he spoke again. "You really don't miss much, do you?"

"I do listen carefully," Billy acknowledged. "It's part of the job, for sure, but I've *always* done it. People take the time to share things they care about with you, seems to me only fair you pay attention."

"Admirable."

"I don't know about that. Point is, after you left Karas's place, it occurred to me that maybe you had, how do shrinks put it? Displaced anger?" Demetrius sat in stunned silence. The pause lasted long enough that Billy grew discomforted and filled the silence. "Sorry," he said. "Never mind."

"No," Demetrius said. "I had the same thought. You're probably right. I was stunned by the way Karas treated that elegant old home, but that doesn't justify being so angry that it spilled onto you."

"No harm, no foul," Billy said with a shrug.

"For you, perhaps. Not for me. In any event, I'll see you at the meeting."

"Okay."

* * *

There were fifteen, maybe twenty, people in the room when Demetrius entered the library for the Town Council's public meeting. He swept the room and saw Billy Williamson chatting with Mark Wells, the woodworker from the swap meet, and Pamela Throop, the Council member who'd saved Demetrius from a sunburn. They were standing near a table that had stacks of handouts.

Demetrius went to the table and examined the papers. He left the financial documents in place but picked up an agenda. He turned and saw a thin woman with frizzy hair; she had an open notepad and a tape recorder on her lap. He moved past her to the row of seats immediately behind hers and, before he sat, snuck a glance at the notepad. It confirmed his guess. "Ms. Irving?" he said.

Virginia turned and gave Demetrius a quick, practiced once-over. "Do I know you?" she asked.

"No, ma'am, we've not met. I am Demetrius Clarke and—"

"Aha! I was planning to leave a message for you with Katherine. You're the writer helping Officer Williamson with the murder investigation, right?"

Demetrius nodded.

"A mystery writer, yes?" Virginia continued. "I thought it might make an interesting feature story, a sidebar to the murder coverage, to do a little human-interest profile about you. You know, going from making it up to investigating the real thing. You up for that?"

"Probably not," Demetrius said.

"No? Come on; it's a good story: big-town writer investigates small-town murder, fiction confronts reality. Plus, I hear you used to live here, right?"

"Small town, indeed," Demetrius said. "Easier to keep a secret in middle school than it is here. I won't even bother to ask how you knew that. Yes, I spent summers here when I was growing up. But no, I'm not particularly interested in being an object for your paper."

"Subject, not object." Virginia's tone was firm. "Subject of a personality profile, if that's a more comfortable concept. Isn't that what LA's all about? Personality, promotion? You don't want to let people know about your books?"

"I prefer not to be a personality in the sense you use it," Demetrius replied. "Of course I want to share my work; that's part of the reason I write. In my experience, however, an occasional review or interview doesn't do much, if anything, to drive sales. It's true, some in my field enjoy some celebrity, but I'm not sure I'm cut out for that kind of exposure." Demetrius thought but didn't say: *And I'm not sure I have the talent, or the luck, to get it in any event.*

"Well, then, how about this? I know I'll never get anything from Officer Williamson or his boss on the Karas murder—blood from a stone. But *you're* not under Shultz's gag order, so maybe—"

"That would be up to Billy," Demetrius said. "I owe it to him to keep his confidence unless he tells me otherwise, so *I* can't be a source, either. At least, not yet."

Irving nodded and jotted a note. She looked up, preparing to say something, when Robert Kraskin rapped his gavel and called the meeting to order. Virginia turned to face the Council, pencil poised at the ready.

Demetrius sat and instantly lost track of what Dr. Kraskin was saying as he reviewed the conversation he'd just had. He and Billy needed good resources to solve a murder. Ginny Irving might well be such an asset, but Demetrius had closed that door. He shook his head slowly, frustrated that he'd been so clumsy and ineffective. He'd been counterproductive, not just in terms of the investigation but in regard to his craft as well; instead of seizing a means of expanding the investigation or his own audience, he'd crushed his chances for either.

The Council meeting was tedious. The back and forth about the budget was cordial and dull, but it moved along at a decent pace under Dr. Kraskin's smooth direction. The members of the Council appeared to be in accord while the townsfolk in the audience gently sniped at them, usually on issues of personal interest. Two or three people wanted to ensure the continued funding of the town's animal shelter, and several people wanted the budget for maintenance and activities at Crandell's Pond to be enhanced.

Demetrius had no investment in the meeting's outcome, so he drifted now and then. He noticed—and liked—the comfort level among the assembly, smiling when someone in the audience directed their questions to "Doc" or "Mark." He also noticed that Ginny Irving had a clever means of taking notes. Instead of trying to capture quotes, when she heard something she wanted to flag, she simply checked the timer on her tape recorder. Rather than jot notes, she just highlighted the comments by their spot on the tape, 1:07, 1:56.

After all the folks in the audience had their say, the Council debated for a few minutes and voted to post the draft budget—with only minor adjustments—on the town website in anticipation of a formal vote at the next official monthly meeting. When the meeting broke up, Ginny Irving stowed her recorder and notes and rose to leave.

"Ms. Irving, a word, please," Demetrius said.

"Yes?"

"I didn't respond well to you earlier, and I want to make

amends," Demetrius said. She raised an eyebrow. "If you really think your readers would be interested in me or my work, I'm game."

"Good."

"There's a price, however."

"What?" Virginia asked.

"I'll trade you. You get your interview, I get to know what you know about Ike Karas's murder."

A tiny smirk appeared on Virginia's face, then vanished. "You got a deal," she agreed.

"What's convenient for you?"

"Sometime tomorrow?"

"I'm free for lunch," Demetrius said. "Let's meet at Crandell's Pond. We can bring our own carryout."

"12:30," Virginia said. "See you then and there."

Chapter 11

BILLY WILLIAMSON ENTERED the hall at Tolland Inn just as Katherine Conrad was putting a plate of blueberry muffins and a butter dish on the dining room table. She invited Billy to join her at the table and settled in, eager to visit at length. Demetrius joined them before Katherine could ask a question.

"Ah, there you are," Billy said. "Good morning, Demetrius." He turned to his hostess. "I don't mean to be rude, ma'am, but I'm here on official business. Mr. Clarke and I need to go over some notes and developments, and some of it is going to be, um . . ."

"Secret? Golly." Katherine's face lit up. "In our little inn? How exciting. By all means, use this room. I should go up and help Lucinda prep some rooms anyway." She poured some coffee into a travel mug and wrapped a muffin in a napkin. She gave Billy an awkward hug as she left. Demetrius got a beaming smile.

"'Developments'? What have you got?" Demetrius inquired.

"Nothing to cheer about, I'm afraid," Billy replied. "I'm not getting anywhere."

"Oh."

"Yeah. Thing is, if Katherine hears that, it'll be all over town in a cocaine heartbeat, and when that happens, it'll get back to Art. I've been avoiding him, and I want to keep it that way until I've got something to report. And . . . I don't."

"Got it," Demetrius said. "Before the meeting last night, I saw you visiting with the two Council members Karas attacked. Were you working the case with them?"

Billy's face betrayed his frustration before he spoke. "Zilch," he said. "Zip, zero."

"Really? No gossip, no guesses about the killer?"

Billy pulled out his notepad, shaking his head. "'Don't know, don't care.' That's from Wells. And 'I haven't heard a thing, and I hope I never do.' That's Throop."

"'Might. Might not.'"

"Huh?"

"Tenny Baker, when I asked her if she would help you."

"See? This is hopeless. Karas had enough enemies to fill Town Hall, but nobody knows anything."

"Or they do, but they don't want you to know about it. Let's look at what we *do* have. Do you know *when* he died? I mean, a precise time?"

"Doc Kraskin told us—Art and me, when we were on the scene—that he figured Karas had been dead for no more than an hour. The doc doesn't have forensic training, but he was confident about that."

"What time did Jimmy deliver the paper?"

"When we interviewed him, he was precise about that: 6:55. Karas is one of the last stops on his route, and Jimmy told us he likes to get done in a hurry so he can get home in time to have breakfast. We got the call from the folks next door as soon as Jimmy alerted them. That was 7:05, so it fits with what Jimmy said."

"So, Karas died between, what, 5 and 6 that morning? Give or take."

"Yes."

"Not a lot of traffic on the street, people on the Green just waking up, maybe getting dressed to get to work, watching some TV news with breakfast. And he died on the deck behind his house, out of sight. Limited pool of potential witnesses."

"Like I say, . . . it's hopeless, Demetrius."

"Okay. Anything new on the cyanide?"

"I checked in with the lab before I came over here," Billy said. "There *is* something, but I don't know how it helps."

"What?"

"Well, first, there's no question it was cyanide. The lab tech says it was a big dose. 'Your victim had enough in him to take out two or three people' is what he said."

"Definitely murder, then," Demetrius said. "A dose that big isn't an accident."

"Lab guy says there's no chance this was anything other than premeditated murder."

"Anything else?"

"Yeah, but I don't know how it helps."

"What?"

"Remember those muffins in the kitchen, the ones we found when we were there? They were all as clean as a whistle."

"No cyanide?"

"Not a hint. The one that killed him is the only one that was poisoned."

"So, he could have died a few days later. It was just chance that he picked the dosed muffin that morning."

"Exactly," Billy confirmed. "Six muffins total. It was just a matter of time."

"Good thing Jimmy got spooked about messing with evidence. Otherwise, he'd be dead, too."

"Yeah. Kid got lucky."

"But Karas didn't. Let's talk about the source," Demetrius suggested. "Where does—"

"Where does cyanide come from?" Billy showed a little pride. "I asked the lab about that 'cause I knew you'd want to know."

"And?"

"Turns out, it's not that hard to come by. Rat poison, insecticide, lawn and garden weed killer—they all have cyanide in them."

"How much would it take?"

"The lab guy laughed about that. He said if the dose Karas got from the muffin had rat poison or weed killer in it, the muffin probably tasted awful."

"But one bite would have been enough?"

"Obviously."

Demetrius sat back and let his gaze drift. Billy topped off his coffee, pulled the butter tray close, and reached for a muffin. He hesitated, his hand in mid-air. Demetrius noticed and broke into laughter. "If you take a bite and die," he said, "I'll give Art a call so he can arrest Katherine."

"Or Jeff," Billy said, grinning. "I can't imagine either of them doing Karas in, but . . ."

"But you never know," Demetrius finished. He selected a muffin, broke off a chunk of its crusty top, drew a deep breath, and popped it into his mouth.

Billy waited a moment before he took the same kind of muffin and applied a pat of butter to it.

"Safety first," Demetrius said. "Okay, if your lab guy is right, then most of the town has access to cyanide, right? When I was in the shed at the far end of the Parish House property, I noticed bags of weed killer and insecticide on a shelf. I can't verify it, but it's a good bet that Tenny Baker's gardener uses that stuff, too—there's not a single weed in her front garden."

"Back to square one, then," Billy said. "Town full of suspects with motive and means, but nobody saw anything, nobody heard anything, nobody knows anything."

"Except the killer."

"Yeah. True that."

"Did Karas keep an appointment book?"

"I didn't find one."

"Did you check his computer? My editor keeps her calendar on her phone, syncs it with her desktop computer."

A look of disappointment crossed Billy's face. "Didn't think of that," he said. "I'll make some time later to check on it."

"Good. Go back, what . . . three, four, five days? See if he had a date with anybody in town, any visitors, a meeting of some sort. Maybe a delivery?"

"I'll see what I can find. Now that you bring it up, Demetrius, there's something else I've been wondering about."

"What?"

"His phone. We didn't find a cell phone. It wasn't on the deck table or his desk, wasn't lying on the kitchen table or his bed stand."

"Maybe in a pocket. What was he wearing when he died?"

"Pajamas, a robe. We checked his pockets before they hauled the body away. Nothing there."

"Hard to imagine he didn't have one," Demetrius said. "With business contacts across the country, the man had to stay in touch, right?"

"I'll search again. Gotta be in his house, doesn't it?"

"Or his car."

"Damn. Didn't think to search it. I'll check today." The men sat in silence for a bit, and then Billy checked his watch.

"Time to patrol," he said. "You want to split another muffin?"

"I shouldn't. But I will."

A look of discovery crossed Billy's face. "Hey," he said, "I know why you knew it was safe to take a bite."

"You do?"

"Yup. Katherine took one when she left. If there's cyanide in 'em, she wouldn't have done that."

"See?" Demetrius smiled. "You're a detective after all."

"Maybe."

"Still," Demetrius said as he winked and pointed at the muffins, "you go first this time."

* * *

"Tell me about *InstanTVision*?"

Virginia Irving had a small salad in a plastic container. Demetrius had a convenience store turkey sandwich and two homemade peanut butter cookies from Katherine's living room snack table. He stopped unwrapping the sandwich and stared at Ginny. "How do you know about that?"

"I'm a reporter," Virginia said. "And I'm not all that bad at it. When I heard you were involved in the Karas investigation, I did some research."

"Oh."

"So, what about *InstanTVision*?"

Demetrius took a bite of his sandwich and chewed very slowly. Virginia waited, nibbling at her salad. "Is this something we have to discuss?" Demetrius asked.

"Why not? You write mysteries, they get published. A couple of months ago, a little blurb in *Variety* reported one of your books was optioned by a production company that had a deal with *InstanTVision* to develop a series based on it."

"Yes, that's true. But—"

"Then, maybe a month later, *Variety* reported that the deal had been abandoned. What happened?"

Demetrius sighed and turned to gaze at the pond. Virginia watched him intently and saw his expression move quickly from frustration to anger and then to calm. "*I* happened," he said. "At least, that's the short answer."

"What's the long one?"

"At the beginning, it was terrific. The production people came to me and asked for permission to pitch the concept to *InstanTVision*. I agreed, and they came back in a hurry with an offer. It was big; they had a deal for an eight-show series with an option for at least two more series after that. To formalize the deal, they optioned the book and any sequels. The offer was more money than I'd made off the book—hell, it was more money than I'd made from all my books. I couldn't resist."

"What went wrong?"

"We'll get there. The book, *She Solves*, is about an ordinary suburban insurance agent who suspects that the death of a client who had a $4 million policy wasn't an accident. The cops and her bosses are sure it was just that, but she knew her client, and what she knew told her otherwise. Her investigation is slow and deliberate and difficult, but she won't give up, and she eventually discovers both a murder plot and the murderer. There are two themes in the book. There's the mystery theme, of course, but she bridles when her superiors and the police dismiss her from the start. They think she's being hysterical, and they scoff and mock her. The deeper she gets into the investigation, the more she relishes the challenge. She's doing her job, but she also grows into a sort of rebel, determined to show them she's not just 'the girl in the office.'"

"So, she's a feminist detective," Virginia noted.

"Yes, but that evolves over time. The crime is fairly

straightforward, but the book is really about the way that sexism permeates the workplace and about her growing awareness of and resistance to it."

"Sounds like something I'd like to read. Or see on TV."

Demetrius snorted and shook his head vigorously. "That's what I thought. That's what the production company thought, too."

"But?"

"Here's how it works. Before they start writing scripts for a new show or series, production companies create something called a 'treatment.' We worked on that—me, the producers, and a screenwriter they'd hired—for a week or two. And when we were satisfied, we went to a meeting with the hotshots at *InstanTVision.*

"The hotshots—a couple of VPs and a production exec—weren't happy. They didn't like that the main character was just an average working woman, a suburban housewife. They wanted her to be, and I'm quoting here, 'a beautiful, sexy, stylish babe with a slightly exotic accent.' Our treatment introduced her leaving her ordinary house and driving an ordinary car to a strip mall insurance office. They wanted to introduce her with a car chase, driving an expensive sports car."

"Uh-oh."

"It got worse. In the book, she's quiet and thoughtful, happily married. They wanted to give her several lovers and a lavish social life. They wanted to dump the modest, middle-class tract house and her husband so she could be independently wealthy with a house on a mountain overlooking the ocean."

Demetrius's eyes grew bright with anger as he continued. "Every time they suggested another change, my side of the table nodded and smiled. They didn't argue, they didn't fight back. Instead, they took copious notes. They were perfectly content, happy even, to throw away the heart of the book—a suburban woman who learns to confront discrimination and develops new strength and power as she proves her misogynist bosses wrong."

Demetrius paused, calming himself, struggling to control his rising volume and acidic tone. "So, the second story you saw wasn't entirely wrong, but it wasn't the real story, either. It was clear to me that the people I'd been working with were eager to get a deal, any deal. But it wasn't a deal I could live with. The show the network wanted is still alive—it's probably going to air next Fall. But it isn't *She Solves*. They didn't abandon the project; I abandoned them."

"And you lost the money."

"That's the craziest part of the story," Demetrius said. "The producers said they wouldn't have done the deal without my book, so they told me to take the money and walk away. Which is exactly what I did."

"So, you're a winner."

"You think so? You think having somebody destroy the integrity of your art, dismiss your work, savage the principles you care about, and do all that while you're sitting at a table with them is winning? It's the worst experience I've had since I started writing, and it has shaken me to my core." Demetrius paused, drew a breath, and let a rueful sigh escape. "I haven't spent a dime of the money, and I'm not sure I will."

"I'm sorry," Virginia said.

"Not as sorry as I am. There's one more piece of the puzzle."

"What?"

"I haven't written a word since those producers first contacted me." Demetrius paused and then caught and held Ginny's eyes. "You really think your readers want to hear that? I can't imagine why."

Virginia took a moment to finish her salad and carefully put the top back on her empty container. "Is that why you're here?"

Demetrius nodded. "Yes. I had to get away, to figure out how to get on with my work or even whether I'm going to. I needed a quiet, safe place where I could think and plan. I've moved around some: college in the Midwest, law school in Boston, and a public defender gig in DC before the firm in LA recruited me. Are you a music fan?"

"I like Broadway showtunes, and I was really into disco for a time."

"I have an Eagles song in mind, about 'a peaceful easy feeling.' That's what Tolland gave me when I spent summers here. It's exactly what I was after when I decided to come back for a visit."

"And you arrived just in time for a murder, Mr. Clarke. You must feel like there's some bad karma following you around."

"To be honest, working with Billy has been something of a relief. All the turmoil and stress I brought with me hasn't gone away, but the Karas thing has been a diversion, and I can't say I'm unhappy about that. It's more amusing than trying to figure out if I belong in the world of fiction, that's for sure."

Virginia nodded. She made a note in her pad and asked Demetrius a series of routine questions—where he'd studied, why he'd left the law, what his books were about—recording his answers with her eye on the recorder's timer. "I think I have what I need," she eventually said, "with one exception."

"Shoot."

"What's your theory of Ike Karas's murder?"

Demetrius smiled and shook his head. "Can't, or maybe won't, comment. I feel obliged to make sure that my help, if I can be helpful, doesn't get Billy Williamson in trouble. He's got a lot riding on this investigation, and, as you know, his boss is not exactly in love with the likes of us."

"*Us?*"

"Writers. Or at least reporters. Shultz isn't aware that I'm lending Billy a hand, but based on what I've heard, he wouldn't like it. So, if you quote me, it'll leave Billy open for some serious trouble, and I don't want that to happen. Besides, I don't have anything for you in any event; there is no 'theory' of the case. We don't have one. All we have are a handful of disconnected facts."

"I understand. I don't like it, but I get it. How about this, then. When you two sort this out, would you be an anonymous source for me? Give me the background, the process that leads to an arrest, and the clues you used, all without attribution. I want the in-depth story once there is one."

"We're back to square one, then," Demetrius said. "I agreed to sit down with you, and you agreed to share what you know about the murder with me. So, what do you know?"

Ginny smiled, a hint of mirth in her eyes. "I don't even know what you do," she said. "I made the deal with you; it's true. But I made it because I was hoping to get something useful from you. I never told you I had anything to offer in exchange, right? Now, neither of us has anything to report about the murder. A fine fix, don't you think, Mr. Clarke?"

"You've done your homework, I assume. Sniffed around, asked questions, tried to run down somebody who knows something?"

"I have. It just didn't get me anything. The cops aren't say-ing 'Boo,' and the whole town seems to be deaf, dumb, and blind when it comes to the good Mr. Karas's demise."

"Maybe *that's* your story," Demetrius suggested. "A murder nobody wants to talk about, never mind solve. A whole town determined to stand mute and look the other way because they didn't like the victim."

Virginia laughed. "You think my editor is going to celebrate when I tell him, 'I got absolutely nothing to report, and that's the story'? I try that, I'll end up covering pet adoptions and PTA meetings for the rest of my life. Not a good career move."

"Yeah. On the other hand, we're sitting on a beach on a perfectly pleasant summer day, kids splashing in the pond, in one of the most delightful little communities anywhere. Maybe we should be grateful for that."

"That and the fact that, when this case gets solved, I'm going to have first crack at the whole story. Right?"

Demetrius smiled. "I didn't agree to that, but I do admire your determination. If I can figure out a way to give you what you're after without doing harm to Billy, you got a deal. Would you like half of this cookie?"

"I was hoping you'd ask."

Chapter 12

DEMETRIUS HAD WALKED from the Inn to his lunch with Virginia Irving. When their meeting ended, he sat on the beach by himself for a few minutes, reviewing their conversation. Then, he stood, tossed his sandwich wrapper in a recycle bin, and started walking back up Cider Mill Road, toward the Green. Rus-D had trod or biked the route hundreds of times as a youngster, never once caring or even noticing that the route had little shade and that the rise of the road made the trip up more demanding than the one going down.

Demetrius plodded along, his mind drifting between Rus-D's charming, innocent summers and the weight of his current burdens. Reliving the *She Solves* saga had been nettlesome, confronting the completely baffling murder in Tolland was frustrating, and, to top it off, the sweat of exertion causing Demetrius's shirt to cling to his back was irritating. His mood darkened as he kept walking, convinced that it was getting hotter with each step he took. He was cursing his decision to leave his car at the Inn when he came to the stone wall along the edge of Parish House. He left the road and leaned against the wall, taking advantage of the sliver of shade the tall trees in the Youngs' backyard provided.

After sitting for a few minutes, Demetrius breathed calmly and used the front of his shirt to wipe the sweat from his forehead. He drifted between his meeting with Virginia and the

Karas murder, lost in thought until a car horn startled him. He thought the sound came from a toy car; instead of a robust toot, it was a cartoonish beep. When Demetrius looked up, he saw Doctor Kraskin in an ancient sports car.

Kraskin waved and doffed his jaunty driving cap. "Need a ride, pal?" he asked.

Demetrius hesitated.

"Oh, come on, Mr. Clarke. It's too hot to be navigating this tarmac on foot, and I'm headed over to Rockville, so I'm gonna drive right past the Inn. You are Clarke, right? Staying at the Inn? Hop in."

Demetrius smiled and moved to the car. "Unless my memory is fading, this is a Triumph Spitfire, isn't it?"

"Right you are. Bought it the day I graduated med school, rewarded myself. We've got a Jeep for winter, but every summer day I can get away with it, I drive this baby. I figure I've paid for it at least four times over. Trust me, when the old girl needs parts, they come dear, but it's worth every dime to be able to drop the top and motor around town. She's got some years on her, but she still knows how to sing."

Kraskin threw the gearshift and pulled away. There was no shuddering or hesitation when he did so; he drove so smoothly that Demetrius sat silent for a moment, admiring the man's skill. "So, the way I hear it, you're staying at the Inn, gathering information for your next mystery novel," Kraskin said.

Demetrius chuckled. "You ever play 'telephone' when you were a kid?"

"Sure. Everybody sits in a circle, the first person whispers something to the next one, the next one whispers to the next, and so on. When the whispers go all the way around the circle, the words the first person said get so distorted that they don't come close to the original."

"That's it. By the time the whisper got to you, the message was garbled. I'm not researching anything. I don't even know if there is a 'next mystery novel.' I was hoping to get away from it all, but somebody killed Ike Karas the day I arrived. Billy Williamson found out who I am and asked me to help him with the investigation. I agreed, although I confess that I haven't done much more than ask obvious questions, and I wouldn't call that 'research.'"

"I see. Billy's a little too fresh to know what those questions should be, I imagine."

"He's doing a credible job, but he's not getting much co-operation from anybody."

"No surprise there." Kraskin came to the intersection at the top of Cider Mill and downshifted twice to slow for the stop sign.

Demetrius nodded his approval. "You drive well, Dr. Kraskin."

"Lots of practice."

"It shows. You were on the scene, weren't you? Confirmed that Karas was dead."

"Yeah. Lucky I didn't get arrested. Art Shultz was there."

"The local troop commander."

"Yup. He's been around for a few years, and I just can't cotton to him. Little too self-important, got an edge on him that irks me. I didn't hide it very well; got a little sassy with him. Credit where it's due, he didn't seem to mind. Or maybe he just ignored me."

"You know what caused the death?"

"Not for sure, 'cause I haven't asked, and nobody's asked me. If they did, I'd guess some kind of poison or an overdose."

"Good guess. Do you treat a lot of the Tolland folk?"

"Fair number. Second generation for a bunch of them, third

109

for a few. I have an office in Rockville, but the town folk know that if there's something serious going on, they can call, and I'll drop by."

"It must be satisfying work, being able to help people you know well."

"Plusses and minuses. I get a kick out of watching the kids grow—some of the young women in this town were toddlers when I met them; now, I deliver their babies. But, of course, I also see my share of misery, cancers and heart failure, sometimes in patients too young to be taken."

The men motored up the hill, passing the Town Hall and gliding along the Green. Tenny Baker was on the sidewalk, heading in their direction and toward her house. Demetrius thought she was a little less upright than usual and figured it was the still air and oppressive summer heat.

Kraskin slowed and tooted, waving. "Good afternoon, Ms. Baker. Good to see you out and about."

"Pay attention to the road, Doctor," Tenny snapped. "When am I not out and about?"

"Never," Kraskin answered.

Demetrius waved at Tenny, and she nodded and then continued down the sidewalk. He turned to Kraskin. "She's quite the lady, isn't she?"

The doctor grinned. "In every sense of the word. Mannered, dainty—even fragile—and the best gossip in town."

"I had pie with her recently. I like her."

"Most do. Good to hear she's welcoming guests, keeping the routine going. Apple, I assume."

"Yes. Delicious, too."

"One of her many skills. She's still baking and taking her walks, so I don't need to worry so much about her. I believe this is your stop, sir." Kraskin pulled over at the entrance to the antique store across the street from the Inn.

Demetrius climbed out and closed his door, leaning on it. "You chair the Town Council, don't you?"

"Somebody has to."

"Between that and your practice, I imagine you know most of the town's residents."

"Probably talked to all of 'em, one time or another."

"So, what do you know about Ike Karas?"

Kraskin laughed richly, then answered. "Two things I know for sure," he said. "Ike Karas was a sonvabitch, and . . . he's dead."

"That's it?"

"Nope. One more thing." The doctor smiled brightly. "I'm pretty sure I didn't kill him. See you around, Clarke."

Kraskin drove away, the little car purring as he made the turn onto the road to Rockville. Demetrius watched him drive off, the doctor's run through the gears in perfect sync with the car's abilities. Then, Demetrius crossed the street and walked into the Inn. Katherine was at her desk with a couple standing in front of her.

"Welcome back, Mr. Clarke. This is Mr. and Mrs. Barsoom. They've come all the way from Seattle—even further away than you. They're joining an East Coast tour this weekend, staying with us until they join the tour in Hartford. I believe they are retired."

Katherine looked up at the couple for confirmation, and they nodded. She continued: "This is Mr. Clarke. He writes mysteries, and he's been staying with us for a few days now. I've put you in the back room with the desk. It has a good view of our backyard and the garden. It's my favorite. If you'd like to leave your bags here, I can have Jeff—Jeff's my husband—carry them up when he's done working in the shed out back. I believe some tours take care of bags for their guests, and I wouldn't want you to think we're any less thoughtful here—wouldn't be good to have folks saying we don't cater to our guests."

"We've packed light," Mrs. Barsoom said. "I'm sure we can manage."

"If you're sure. There's fresh lemonade on the table in the living room if you'd like to sit for a bit before you go up. And we have appetizers and wine later, early evening. I certainly hope you'll join us for that. We think of it as a sort of extended family gathering, all our guests sharing with one another, the way aunts and uncles and cousins and such do, you know?"

Mrs. Barsoom gave her husband a sharp look. "Let's go, dear," she said. And then, turning to Katherine, "Thank you. We'll think about joining you this evening, but I need to go decompress from our flight."

Before Katherine could answer, Mrs. Barsoom grabbed a bag with one hand and her husband with the other and moved rapidly up the stairs and out of sight. Demetrius waited a beat before he followed them, nodding but not speaking to Katherine as he left.

* * *

Billy Williamson went through every desk drawer, every kitchen cabinet and drawer, the cloak closet downstairs, the walk-in closets in Karas's bedroom suite, and all the jacket and pants pockets he could find. He checked inside the collection of shoes. He fished around beneath the cushions of the couches and the leather chairs. He checked the back patio. He found the keys to Karas's car on a hook and went to the driveway where it was parked, checking the glove box, the door panel storage spaces, the back seats, the two bucket seats in front, and the trunk. When Billy was fishing around under the two front seats, he skinned two knuckles. He checked the front porch, the kitchen pantry, and, just to be sure, both guest bedrooms and the bathroom that separated them.

Ike Karas's cell phone was not anywhere.

Frustrated and tired, Billy carefully closed and locked the house and walked over to his cruiser, parked behind Karas's Cadillac. As he was about to climb in, he heard a short burst from a siren immediately behind him. He jumped a little and turned to see Art Shultz pull into the driveway, blocking it. "Over here, Williamson," Art demanded. "I need a report from you; been waiting for days."

Billy's shoulders slumped, and, for just a second, he thought about jumping into his cruiser and driving across the front lawn to escape. As if reading his mind, Shultz said, "Here, Williamson. Now."

"I've been meaning to catch up with you, sir," Billy began. "Somehow, we keep missing each other. I'm in the office when you're not, then you're there but I'm not."

"You don't have a phone?"

"I figured in person would be better, so I was just—"

"Stalling. Enough of this, kid. How close are you to arresting somebody for murdering Ike Karas?"

"Well—"

"I know what the lab said. The man was poisoned. Cyanide. Have you checked with shops in Rockville, maybe Vernon, too? Anybody buy an oversized order of insecticide? Rat poison?"

"No, sir."

"No suspicious purchases or no, you haven't even checked?"

Billy blushed. "I haven't checked, sir. The thing is, just

113

about everybody in town keeps a supply of that stuff in garages, basements, sheds. Whoever did this probably had what they needed at hand, and besides, there's nothing unusual about stocking up on weed killer in the middle of summer."

"Karas spent a lot of money to get that Throop woman and that woodworker, what's his name—"

"Mark Wells."

"Yes, Wells, thrown out of office. That's a pretty good motive. You talked to them?"

"At the budget meeting, sir. Neither one of them knows anything, or at least, they aren't talking. The fact is, sir, most people in town don't want to talk about the murder. Everywhere I go, it's another dead end."

"We don't accept dead ends," Shultz said. "We're close to closing the book on the homicides over in Stafford Springs. I don't want to do it, but I can assign one of the senior detectives to this case. I can do that now. You can go back to patrolling, let somebody else take over. How's that sound?"

Billy pulled himself up to his full height and drew a deep breath. "To be honest, sir, it sounds lousy."

"I don't want a murder in my jurisdiction going cold, Williamson. It'll look bad, give the brass in Hartford reason to wonder what the hell we're doing out here in the sticks. What are you looking at now? Why are you back here?"

"His phone, sir. We can't find his phone anywhere. We figure there could be some information in it, give us a lead. You know, a calendar, phone calls coming in or going out just before he was killed. It could be a valuable resource, but it's gone missing."

"Whaddya mean, 'we'?"

Billy swallowed hard and coughed a little to cover it. He pulled a tissue out of a pocket and brought it to his mouth, loudly clearing his throat.

"Somebody else working this case, Williamson? Some insurance guy sniffing around, wondering how to handle a life insurance payment? That broad, works for the paper? She been sticking her nose in? We don't want that."

"No, sir," Billy replied, trying to summon a note of confidence. "I know we don't talk to the press about open cases. I wouldn't do that. As far as I know, nobody from an insurance company is involved, either."

"Good. Keep it close, kid. Last thing I want is somebody chattering about how we can't solve a simple murder. Maybe it is time to bring in somebody else."

"I can solve this, sir. I want to solve this. I just need more time."

"How much?"

"I can't say, sir. Most folks around here seem to think it was a good thing, taking Karas out. He wasn't popular, and he stirred people up."

"So, you've got plenty of suspects."

"A town full of them, sir."

"Find the killer."

"I'm working on it, sir, every spare minute I've got. Been putting in overtime on it."

"Work harder. Shake the trees, beat the bushes, threaten these yokels if you have to. I want results."

"Believe me, sir, so do I."

"Then get me something. Yesterday. I'll give you a few more days, you hear? You don't turn something up right quick, I'm going to move somebody else over."

"I hear you, chief."

"Time's running out for you, Williamson. The clock is ticking. Next time we talk, it had better be about a warrant or an arrest. You hear me?"

"Yes, sir."

"Get it done. I want results."

"Yes, sir."

Shultz threw his car in reverse and hammered his accelerator, throwing up dust and grit as he raced down the drive and onto the street.

Billy slumped against the fender of his cruiser, shaking just a little. He climbed in behind the driver's seat and gripped the wheel. As his tension eased, he allowed himself a small smile. "Demetrius Clarke is working this case as hard as I am, sir," he said to his dashboard. "I may have forgotten to mention that."

Chapter 13

D EMETRIUS SKIPPED THE communal breakfast at the
Inn. Instead, he slipped downstairs and grabbed a cup of
coffee from the urn and carried it back to his room. He sat in
the chair by the window and responded to a few emails on his
laptop before he set it aside and settled in to read Rex Stout.

He was a quarter of the way into *A Knock on the Door*, one
of his favorites, when there was a tap on his door. He was
setting the book aside when the door opened, and a sturdy
young woman in jeans and a tee shirt walked in, leaving a
rolling cart at the door and dragging a sizable vacuum cleaner
behind her.

"Come on in," Demetrius said. "You must be Lucinda."

The woman didn't respond and, initially, didn't even notice
Demetrius was in the room. Bright neon orange wires ran from
a back pocket in her jeans to a set of headphones, also orange.
She was humming to herself. When she looked around the
room and finally spotted Demetrius, she blushed. "I'm so sorry,
sir, I didn't realize . . ." She draped the headphones around her
neck. "I thought you'd be out already."

"No problem," Demetrius replied. "I'm just enjoying a
busman's holiday." He stood and slipped on a pair of loafers.
He laid his book on the table, folded down his laptop, and
moved toward the door. "I'll get out of your way," he said.

"I can come back later." The woman pulled a stylish black

phone out of her pocket and hit a few keys. The muted sound of her music emanating from the headphones—Demetrius thought it might be the Who or Pink Floyd—stopped.

"No need," Demetrius said. "I'm happy to leave you to it. Some fresh air would be welcome, and it looks like it's another beautiful summer day."

"Too warm for me. Thank you, sir. I won't be long."

"Take all the time you need. And thanks for taking care of the room for me. You make the bed as tight as a drum. I'm lousy at that."

The woman smiled. "Had a lot of practice. Plus, Ms. Conrad's pretty strict about that. She says there's no good reason to do a bad job."

"She's not wrong about that," Demetrius agreed. "Thanks again. Nice to meet you."

The woman nodded, punched her phone, and put the headphones back on. She was humming again when Demetrius pulled the door shut.

Demetrius went out the Inn's front door and looked up and down the Green. He saw a woman across the street, standing in the doorway to the antique shop. He went to the curb, waiting for a few cars to motor by before he crossed the street and went into the shop.

"Good morning!" the woman said, holding the door open for Demetrius. "Welcome to my shop. Do please come on in. I'm Suzy Henderson," she said, extending her hand.

Demetrius shook Suzy's hand. "Demetrius Clarke," he said. "I'm staying just across the street at—"

"At the Inn. I hear you used to live here, so you probably know that this place—"

"Yes, this place was a Red & White store. Basic grocery supplies, canned goods, a small butcher case, laundry supplies, paper goods. There was a single gas pump out front, too."

"That's right," Suzy confirmed. "It was owned by—"

"It was owned and operated by Harold Clough. It's the first place I ever worked, eight maybe nine years old. I'd come in right after he opened, and he'd let me stock the shelves, sweep the floor. He paid me 50 cents for each chore."

Suzy Henderson gave Demetrius a thorough once-over, smiling brightly. "Tenny said you spent a lot of summers here. Are you enjoying your stay?"

"I am," Demetrius answered. He stepped around Suzy and moved to the center of the shop. He turned slowly around, concentrating not on the slapdash collection of antiquities she had on display but focusing instead on the shape and the light and the aroma of the place. "I usually spent what Harold paid me as soon as I got it," he said. "I'd get a bottle of pop from the cold box on the porch. I liked Fanta Orange most. I doubt the one you've got out there is the same machine."

"No," Suzy said. "I picked up the one out there at an auction just a month or so ago."

"Well, Harold's looked just like that. If I earned enough, I'd get a candy bar or a package of cupcakes and sit on the stoop. I'd get up bright and early almost every morning during one of my summers here so I could bike up to this store right after breakfast and see if Harold had something for me to do. He usually did, but even when he didn't, he'd visit with me in between customers. I don't remember what we talked about, but I do recall that he didn't talk to me like a kid. I felt grown up when I was with him."

Demetrius wandered around the shop, examining knick-knacks and dishware and old photographs and, in one section, several rocking chairs and small tables. The floor groaned in places as he moved, and he smiled when it did. "Creaky floors," he said. "My family was in what you folks call Parish House now, and when I visited there a few days ago, I knew how the floors would groan before I walked on them. Same thing here. It's musical, don't you think?"

"Honestly, Mr. Clarke, I guess I never noticed. Mostly, I just fret over how to keep the floor clean and where to put things."

Demetrius moved slowly around the shop. Suzy went to a counter and began shuffling papers around, leaving him free to meander and browse. He sensed she had concluded that he wasn't going to buy anything and imagined that a lot of those who came into her shop were like that—interested and amused but not necessarily shopping. Suzy glanced up now and then and watched Demetrius pause over items, deep in thought.

"I discovered the joys, and the oddities, of English in this store," Demetrius said.

Suzy wasn't sure if he was talking to her or himself, so she hesitated for a moment before she said, "I understand you're a writer."

"I am," Demetrius confirmed. "Or at least, I have been up to now."

"That's something," Suzy said. "I can barely manage a good letter myself, so I've always admired people who can write well. I don't quite understand, though. How did this place get you started?"

"Harold's last name," Demetrius said. "C-l-o-u-g-h. It didn't make sense to me. I thought the way it was pronounced should rhyme with 'though,' so it sounded like Clo or maybe 'plough,' so it would be Clow. But Harold pronounced it so that it rhymed with 'enough' or 'rough'—his name was Harold 'Cluff.' That didn't seem logical to me even after I learned to pronounce it properly, and I spent some time trying to make

120

sense of it. I asked my dad to explain it to me, but all he said was, 'English doesn't always work the way you expect it to.' I've been sort of fascinated with that ever since. Add an 'e' and 'cur' turns into 'cure,' but add an 'e' to 'sing' and you get 'singe'—it's all sort of whimsical, isn't it?"

"I guess so," Suzy said, though her look implied that she felt otherwise.

Demetrius walked over to the collection of chairs and tables and moved among them. He found a wooden sign on a tabletop, picked it up, and observed what was painted onto it:

Tolland
Established 1722

The wood was distressed and rough and the painted letters faded, but it didn't appear to be weather-beaten. "This isn't an original, is it?" Demetrius asked.

Suzy smiled. "No. It's contemporary. Mark Wells made it. He does several like that, makes them look older by hammering the wood and using a stain to give them a kind of patina. I carry them for him on consignment."

"I'll take it," Demetrius said. "How much?"

"For you, ten bucks. If you'd like, I can have it shipped for you. Tenny says you live out in California."

"I do," Demetrius said, "but I don't want it shipped there. It's a gift. It's not going to leave Tolland." He carried it to the counter and laid it down, pulling out his wallet and extracting some cash.

"Feel free to wander around some more." Suzy pointed to a doorway on her left. "There's a back room with more furniture and artwork. It used to be—"

"It used to be Harold's storage area. I hauled boxes from back there to the shelves in this room."

121

"Exactly. Go on back, have a look around."

"Thanks, I will."

Demetrius spent some time in the back room, imagining shelves and stacks of boxes with canned peas and pickle relish and pasta and bars of soap. He admired a sturdy, ornate dining set that appeared to be at least a hundred years old, a wooden foot stool shaped like a cloverleaf, and a cigar box with a brass plate that said: *Happy Holidays, Traveler's Insurance, Hartford.* Demetrius lingered in the shop for most of an hour before he retrieved his purchase. Suzy had expertly wrapped the sign in brown paper, securing it with string rather than tape. Demetrius thanked her before he left and walked down the sidewalk toward Parish House.

When Demetrius knocked on the door to Parish House, he heard Meryl Young shout, "Abby, sees who's at the door! I'm finishing the dishes, and your mom's on a conference call. Make sure you know who it is before you open the door, right? If it's a stranger, come get me, okay?"

"Okay," Abby agreed.

"Hello, Abby. It's me, Demetrius Clarke. I had dinner with you a few days ago."

"Yes, of course," Abby said. "I know you. You had a bicycle, just like me. You know Kanga and Roo, too."

"That's exactly right. You have a very good memory." Demetrius heard the young girl fumble with the latch on the door before it opened just an inch or two, and she peered out.

"It *is* you!" Abby exclaimed. "Please come in." When Demetrius did, Abby smiled at him and raced down the entry hall. "Daddy, it's that nice man, the one who lived in my room!"

Meryl Young came out of the kitchen and met his guest in the dining room. He had a damp towel draped over one shoulder and another in his hand. "Hey! Welcome back, Mr. Clarke.

Sorry I can't shake; I'm all wet."

"That's okay. I brought you a present."

"Really? No need for that. Stay here, would you? I'll go see if Janice is done with her call." Meryl turned to his daughter. "Abby, stay with Mr. Clarke so he doesn't get lonely, okay?"

"Okay." Abby walked to stand next to Demetrius. "Do you have a cat?"

"No. I don't have any pets."

"I want a cat."

"They're good companions."

"Mommy says 'No.' She says I'm not old enough to take care of a cat, but I think I am. Do you?"

"I don't know, but your mom probably knows best, don't you think?"

Abby frowned. "Maybe."

"Mr. Clarke, how nice to see you," Janice greeted him. She was smartly dressed, and her smile was warm. She removed an earpiece as she approached him. "I was talking to New York. What brings you here?"

"I have a gift," he answered, holding up the package.

"Oh, that's so kind. You really didn't need to. We enjoyed having you here."

"Not as much as I did being here," Demetrius said. "You and your family put me back in touch with a part of my life I hold very dear. This is the least I could do." He handed Janice the package. "Maybe Abby could open it for you?"

Janice laughed and handed the package to Abby. Abby untied the bow and wrapped the string around her neck, then tore at the paper with energetic enthusiasm. When she saw what was inside, her face fell a little. "That's not a toy," she said, dejected.

"No, I'm afraid not," Demetrius confirmed. "At least, not for you. It's just for fun, though. It's for your parents."

"I love it," Meryl said. "Maybe we can hang it right under the Parish House plaque out front."

"Or here in the dining room," Janice suggested. "It's rustic; it'll fit right in. Thank you, Demetrius. How thoughtful."

"I saw it at the antique store and thought of you. A trifle, really. The truth is, I also wanted to leave something behind—something from me to celebrate, or maybe commemorate, my time here."

"Stay for lunch?" Meryl inquired, taking the sign and turning it over, examining it. "Vintage look but probably not an antique. Mark Wells, maybe?"

"Good guess," Demetrius said. "Lunch would be welcome if it's not too much trouble."

Janice laughed. "No trouble at all," she said. "In summer, when I can get away from my phone and my computer, Abby and I have picnics in the backyard. Shall we do that today, Abby?"

"Oh, let's!"

"Perfect. Meryl, you organize some drinks for us. There's cold cider and lemonade in the fridge. Abby and I will get some sandwich stuff together."

"Can Kanga come, too?" Abby pleaded.

"I certainly hope so," Demetrius said.

The two men organized a pitcher and plastic cups and went out to the large yard beyond the rose garden. There were several Adirondack chairs and a low table beneath the tall trees on the side of the yard, so they sat in partial shade.

"I thought you were just here for a long weekend," Meryl said.

"Billy Williamson persuaded me to hang around a bit longer," Demetrius said. "But I would have extended my stay in any event. I didn't want to ignore an invitation from Tenny Baker. I think she might have cast a spell on me if I didn't visit with her."

Meryl grinned. "Near as I can tell, she's fully capable of wreaking havoc if she's peeved. She's a living legend, that gal. She knows more about this town than the rest of us combined, including the preservationist crowd. They'd never admit that, of course. They're true believers, those folks. They're always right, too—just ask them."

Demetrius leaned forward. "They've been on my mind, actually," he said. "Billy and I aren't making much progress with Karas's murder. Billy tells me that the exchanges between him and that group were not exactly cordial."

"You think one of them murdered him?"

"I haven't any idea."

Meryl leaned back and sipped his drink before speaking again. "It's true that they were up in arms over Karas's plan to tear down that house, but the phrase is purely metaphorical, if you ask me. They're what my students would call 'nerds' or 'dweebs,' well-informed but not quite there, you know? Active, but only in the talk-you-to-death sense. In my view, the only way they'd do anybody harm would be by burying them in documents and long, long letters with footnotes."

Abby joined them, carefully carrying a tray with paper plates and plastic utensils. She set it down on the table and met Demetrius's eyes. "Kanga will be right here," she said. "Kanga had to wait 'cause I couldn't carry her and all this stuff." She raced back toward the house, skipping past her mother carrying a second tray.

"Jan, Demetrius wonders if our enlightened preservationist neighbors might have murdered Karas."

"Why? They got what they wanted, didn't they?" Janice asked.

"Half of it," Demetrius replied. "Karas couldn't touch the exterior, but he did his best to create the house he wanted to build inside." Demetrius described what he'd seen: the open first floor with its wall of glass facing the backyard, the ultra-modern kitchen, and the penthouse apartment style of the second floor.

"I had no idea," Meryl said. "You can't tell from the outside, can you? The guy really was a philistine, wasn't he?"

"What's that, daddy?" Abby was nibbling at a sandwich that she pretended to share with her stuffed companion.

"A man with lots of power and very little wisdom or kindness," Meryl said.

"Oh."

They ate and chatted. Demetrius shared news of his visits to the pond. Meryl and Janice both knew Pamela Throop, and they knew Virginia Irving's work but hadn't met her. Demetrius also informed his hosts that he'd been to the Town Council meeting and noted that neither Meryl nor Janice had attended.

"The people who sit on the Council change from time to time," Janice said, "but their direction doesn't. Unless something extraordinary comes up, the meetings are pretty much the same, month after month, year after year."

"Karas was the extraordinary when he got here," Meryl said. "We went to those meetings, but so did just about everybody in town. It was quite the show. It's no wonder the murder is so opaque; I'd peg anybody who went to any of those shouting matches as a suspect."

"That's the problem," Demetrius said.

"Maybe it's the *answer*," Janice suggested. She giggled, and there was a mischievous twinkle in her eye.

Demetrius raised an eyebrow. "How do ya mean?"

"Agatha Christie," Janice continued. "*Murder on the Orient Express*?"

Both men laughed. "Brilliant," Demetrius said. "So, the whole town did it."

"A vast conspiracy," Meryl said. "Instead of a train full of killers, it's a town full of suspects."

Abby raised her hand. "Me, too? Can I be a suspit, too?"

Meryl gave Abby an exaggerated look. "Of course not," he said. "Everybody knows that small children don't murder people."

"Oh, phooey." Abby held up her companion. "How about Kanga?"

"Absolutely not," Demetrius said. "Nobody in the Hundred Acre Wood ever hurt anybody. They can't be suspits 'cause they're all good friends."

"And we all know Mr. Karas didn't have any of those," Meryl asserted.

"I still like my theory," Janice said. "A dozen or more Tollanders get together and hatch their plot, and they all swear to silence. Everybody is guilty, but if you ask any of them, they're all innocent."

"I'll give you this," Demetrius said. "That theory makes more sense than anything else we've got."

They finished their food. Abby was dispatched to the kitchen to return with a plate of homemade cookies for dessert. "Mommy made 'em," she announced. "I helped, didn't I?"

"You certainly did," Janice said.

"That must be why they taste so good, Abby," Demetrius said. "May I have another?"

"You have to ask Mommy."

"Please," Janice said, "have another. You too, little one."

"An extra cookie?"

"Just this once."

"Boy," Meryl said, "talk about major crimes. The kid gets another cookie, but I don't."

"She can afford it," Janice said, winking. "*You* can't."

On his way back to the Inn, Demetrius passed Tenny Baker's house. She was sitting in a rocker on her front porch. The rocker was still, her eyes were closed, and her face was pale and drawn. As he watched, her head slowly drooped to one side, and Demetrius was struck by her age. Dozing in the sun, she seemed to be slowly crumbling under the weight of her years. Her wide front yard separated Demetrius from her porch, but he stepped lightly just to be certain he didn't disturb her rest.

Chapter 14

"MARK WELLS SPENT close to a hundred bucks on weed killer ten days ago. I'm going to question him in about half an hour." Billy was sitting in his cruiser in the parking lot in front of the Tolland Family Restaurant, his phone cradled on his shoulder. He was nursing coffee and scrambled eggs in a Styrofoam container. The coffee was tepid, the eggs not even that.

"Seriously, Billy? I know you don't have a lot to work with, but he seems so unlikely. What brought this on?" Demetrius was in the backyard at the Inn, sitting in one of Jeff Conrad's chairs. He had been reading when his phone rang, but a collection of clouds had begun dancing across the morning sun, and the shifting light was distracting. So, he didn't mind the interruption.

"Shultz," Billy said. "He caught up with me at Karas's house and read me the riot act about the lack of progress. He suggested—that's putting it mildly, if you get my drift—that I find out who's been buying products with cyanide in them. I made some calls, mostly just to satisfy Shultz. But when somebody buys that much weed killer . . ."

"I get it. Well, at least you can satisfy your boss that you did what he wanted. I think you'll come up empty, but I guess it's worth a try."

"Nothin' else going on."

"True. So, if you want my opinion—"

"Of course, I do, Demetrius. It's why I called."

"I'd ask him the only question that matters."

"'Did you kill Karas?'"

Demetrius laughed. "That'd do it if he's compulsively honest or so guilty he can't stand it any longer. But the question I have in mind is a bit more subtle. Ask him if he knows how to bake."

"Knows how to . . . oh, I get it. Muffins."

"Muffins."

"Good idea."

"We'll see. Did you tell Shultz about me?"

"No way. He'd probably fire me on the spot if he thought I couldn't handle this on my own."

"Just making sure we're still underground. Given the town grapevine, I'm not sure he'll be in the dark much longer in any event. Anyhow, let me know how it goes with Wells, okay?"

"Of course."

Billy had another bite of eggs and climbed out of his cruiser. He tossed the container, leftover eggs and all, into a trash can and went into the restaurant to freshen his coffee. Rather than trouble the young woman behind the counter, he served himself. She looked over when he did and smiled.

"Savin' me some steps, Billy? Right nice of you. Thanks."

"My pleasure, Katie. See you tomorrow."

Billy drove to Cross Farms Recreation Center. It was lightly populated, but a few kids were playing catch on one of the ball fields, their mothers watching from a shaded area, sharing coffee and an animated conversation. There were three baseball fields in the park: two regulation-sized and one smaller one for littlest Little League and T-ball play. Mark Wells was sitting on a bench near the mini-field. He was wearing bib overalls, and his feet were propped up on a wheelbarrow. When he saw Billy approach, he moved slowly but gracefully to his feet, gave the shovel and rake handles sticking out of the wheelbarrow wide berth, and extended his hand. Billy took it and removed his trooper hat.

"Sorry to bother you, Mr. Wells, but we're still trying to sort out the death of Ike Karas, and I have some questions for you."

"Call me Mark, Billy. It's not like we're strangers, right? You think I had something to do with that bast— That miserable excuse for a human being's death?"

"The investigation is still open. He was poisoned, so we're running down some folks who had access to it."

"Hemlock? Snake venom? Sorry, Billy, but I don't have access to stuff like that. Wouldn't know how to get access, either, comes down to it."

"Cyanide, Mr. Wells."

"Mark."

"Mark. Cyanide killed him."

"Don't have access to that, either."

"Folks over at Garden Barn say you do."

"The shop in Rockville? They say that? I'll be damned. They must be confused. I didn't know they sell cyanide, and I sure didn't buy any."

"They say you did. Let me ask you something, Mark. Do you know how to bake?"

Wells burst into laughter. "You're kidding, right? I barely know how to boil water. You want to check that out, ask Lois. She says I'm so out of place in our kitchen that pots and pans run for cover when they hear me coming. I'm not the worst cook in Tolland, but that's 'cause I can't cook at all."

Billy smiled and nodded. "Okay. Let me ask you this, then:

131

what do you need with so many sacks of weed killer?"

"Why on earth— Oh, wait. You tellin' me that weed killer has cyanide in it?"

"Exactly."

"Didn't know that. Guess I oughta start reading labels, huh? That the stuff that killed Karas? Weed killer? Some sort of poetic justice there, you ask me—the guy was the only weed on the Green, that's for sure."

"Mark, I have to ask again. You bought more weed killer than most folks use in a year, is what they told me at Garden Barn. The kid who waited on you said they had to use a flatbed trolley to get six sacks of it to your car. Why so much?"

Wells held up both hands, grinning. "You caught me, Officer. Guilty as charged. Cuff me, I'll go quietly. I snuck into Karas's house and spread weed killer all over the place. Then, just to make sure it worked, I held him down and poured an entire stack of the stuff down his throat. You wanna read me my rights?"

"Come on, Mark, this is serious. I have to know—"

Mark reached over and took Billy's arm. "Follow me."

Wells led Billy onto the pint-sized ball field, across the neatly manicured infield, and out onto the open swath of grass in left field, which reached all the way to a fence. He stopped about halfway between third base and the outfield fence and swept his arm across the swath. "See that, Billy?" he asked. "Left and left center, then center and right."

"I know what a baseball field looks like."

"I would hope so," Wells said, "it's the great American game. What do you see out here, Billy?"

"The outfield."

"Well, yeah, for sure. But look around and tell me, you see any weeds?"

Billy started in the corner of right field and checked out the whole area until he was looking down the third base line.

"No," he said. "No weeds."

"You got that right, kiddo. Let's go over there behind that dugout." The men walked across the outfield and onto the grass in foul territory until they came to a cement dugout. Wells led him to an area between the dugout and metal bleachers where two trash cans and a recycle bin sat. Wells flipped the top of the recycle bin open. "Check it out," he said.

Billy leaned over and peered in. He saw half a dozen soda cans, a sizable collection of empty plastic water bottles, and six empty sacks of weed killer. "I'm not saying I'm losing sleep over Karas's death, Billy," Wells said, "and I surely do like the idea of using weed killer to do the job, but as you can see—out there in the field and right here in this trash can—I used your alleged murder weapon to maintain the best damn Little League ball yard in town."

Billy shuffled his feet and stared at the ground for a moment. "Geez, this is awkward. Sorry to trouble you, Councilman. Like I say, the investigation is open, so we got to check everything. I guess I can cross you off my list."

"Hey, I appreciate your diligence, Billy. We all know you're a good cop. Truth is, I'm glad to know you're working so hard on this. I could say I'm sorry I can't be more helpful, but I can't 'cause I don't know anything about it."

"Neither does anybody else," Billy said. "Thanks for your time."

"Sure," Mark replied. "See you at the next Council meeting. Be good now, you hear?"

Later that day, Billy spent some time completing a report to Art Shultz. It didn't contain a whit of evidence or a hint of resolution, but he hoped it might buy him a little more time. To help his hope along, he made specific reference to the fact that his interview with Wells was the direct by-product of Shultz's astute direction.

* * *

Demetrius Clarke left the backyard at the Inn and strolled down the sidewalk to the library. From the Green, it was as he remembered it, a stately old brick building built to last. He could see an addition on the back side of the structure, which was far more contemporary, although it blended well with the original.

Inside, Demetrius was dismayed to find that it wasn't at all like the building he had visited once a week without fail when he was a child. While he'd spent his time on his bike and at the pond, the library had been part of Rus-D's life as well; his parents had insisted that, summer vacation or not, he would read. He remembered wandering the aisles, sometimes in search of a book he'd been told to read but, just as often, on his own, to explore. He remembered reading a series of biographies—Sam Wannamaker, Thomas Jefferson, a couple of civil war generals—that had been bound in orange covers and had been easy reading. The shelves had been full and the lighting relatively muted. The quiet of the large room was a little ominous for Rus-D, but it was also calming, comfortable.

The library's new interior, which a placard told Demetrius was completed in 1981, was bright and airy. A large section for children had been added, as had a meeting room. It was modern and open and welcoming, but for Demetrius, it was also faintly sad; while he was pleased to see that the building had been expanded and enhanced, he felt a twinge of loss for what had been.

Demetrius searched for a card catalog and found none. Instead, computer stations had replaced little cards in tiny filing cabinet drawers. He sat at a screen and entered the titles of his own work; none were cataloged. He hadn't expected to find his name or titles—his work hadn't cracked the library sales ceiling—but confirming that didn't improve his mood. He moved on and found that the catalog did include digital files from the Vernon *Journal Inquirer*, and after a brief search, he landed on a series of stories, all under Virginia Irving's byline, about the controversy over Ike Karas's proposal to raze his house.

The stories Demetrius reviewed charted the progress of Karas's proposal: hearings, testimony from experts on both sides of the controversy, staff reports, more hearings, votes. Demetrius scanned them all. The reporting, deliberately balanced and energetic, merely confirmed what Demetrius already knew, that the uproar over what the town's preservationists called "the desecration of the Green" had been fierce and fulsome. He didn't take notes but did pay attention to the names of those most often quoted.

Karas himself had spoken frequently, supported by the experts on zoning and land use he had retained. A woman named Denise Grantham had been a vocal opponent, and her husband, Glen, had served as a volunteer lawyer for the opposition. At each public hearing, Tenny Baker had offered observations that Virginia couldn't resist quoting: "Mr. Karas has so little respect for heritage that we have to assume he was poorly educated" and "Allowing this travesty to proceed will surely ruin everything about our village." Richard Groom, the Tolland town manager, had provided chapter and verse about sections of the town's code that "clearly prevent" the changes Karas proposed.

When he was done with the articles, Demetrius felt he'd learned little that he didn't already know, although he had some interest in the Granthams, whose names he'd not heard before. Still, he thought the exercise took more time than it was worth.

Demetrius left and walked down the Green toward Karas's house. When he came to the little cottage where Zoey Caldwell lived, he spotted a woman in a house dress working on a patch of flowers that bordered the front of the house. He watched her for a few moments and then crossed her lawn. "Ms. Caldwell?"

The woman turned to face Demetrius. Her gray hair was cut in a buzz, a style which made her appear younger than she obviously was. Her glasses were so large that they dominated her face, and there was a smudge of dirt on her forehead. "No solicitors," she said.

Demetrius smiled. "I'm not selling anything, ma'am. I just wanted to introduce myself. I'm Demetrius Clarke, and a long time ago, I spent my summers here in Tolland. You and Ms. Baker are the only two who live on the Green who were here back then."

Zoey took a few steps toward Demetrius, squinting in the sun to evaluate him. "Rus-D, isn't it? You're Beth Church's nephew. Your mom grew up here, too, I believe . . . in Parish House. Do I have that right?"

"You do. Quite the memory, I must say."

"It's a curse. I've got so much useless information floating around that I get easily distracted. It frustrates me, having to shove all the nonsense aside in order to focus on what matters."

"Ah. I believe you're a writer?"

"I am," Zoey confirmed. "Nonfiction and essays, culture and social trends. I freelance, although I write newsletters for a handful of nonprofits to keep food on the table. It's a hard-knock life, as Annie's orphan friends would say."

"I know," Demetrius said. "I write fiction—mysteries—

and it's a rare month when that puts food on my table without some supplemental income from my savings. I wanted to greet you because when I was a lad, my folks used to talk about how dedicated you were, determined to make a living. I have a vague memory that you found your way into *The New Yorker*, and my dad thought that made you an exceptional talent. It sounded like an exciting life, writing. It intrigued me."

Zoey shaded her eyes with a garden-gloved hand, adding to the smudge. She looked at Demetrius for several moments, not speaking. He feared he'd said something wrong.

"Have I offended you, ma'am? I certainly didn't intend—"

Zoey waved Demetrius off. "Don't be silly. It's true that when I was younger, I managed to do a couple of profiles that garnered some attention, but they were few and far between. It didn't last long, and I settled into a rut rather quickly. Features in obscure magazines, an occasional commissioned assignment, and a lot of what I call 'bread-and-butter' work—not very inspiring but vital to my survival."

"Do you still enjoy it? The writing, I mean."

"I do," Zoey said, "although I don't have the fire I once did. Do you?"

"Have the fire?"

"No. Enjoy it."

Demetrius thought it over and said, "I do. It gives me joy. I don't like the business of it, the competition and the tedium of trying to generate sales and the agents and editors who want to change the work so it's more 'marketable.' But when I'm not consumed with that stuff, the actual writing—crafting a plot, finding just the right word, creating characters I like—that's all fun."

"Then you're a writer!" Zoey said. "I'd welcome you to the club that I'm not sure anybody in their right mind would want

137

to join."

"My membership may be temporary in any case," Demetrius said.

"Blocked?"

"No, just without direction right now. That's why I'm here. I thought visiting Tolland again might help, maybe put me back on the right path. I had an unpleasantness about one of my books recently. It soured me, so I thought coming back here would help to leave the sour and find the sweet."

"'Sweet.' That's Tolland, all right. It's why I've never given up this old house. Being here is comforting. It's quiet and contemplative. I have a nice little rent-controlled apartment in New York, but as often as I can, I escape. That 'business' side does corrode one; you're right about that. Still, for my part, I've never thought about doing anything else."

"*I* have. I did, in fact. I may go back to my 'anything else.' I'm here mostly because I'm trying to figure it all out."

Zoey nodded.

"Anyhow," Demetrius continued, "I won't keep you from your gardening. I just wanted to meet you. You were a sort of role model for me when I was a kid. Being a writer seemed, I don't know, appealing? Rebellious? *Romantic*."

Zoey smiled. "Romantic, as in fickle and foolish and fraught with frustration, Mr. Clarke? That about sums up my life."

"Mine, too," Demetrius said.

Zoey turned and bent over her flower bed, surveyed her choices, and snapped off a big bright daisy. "Here," she said, handing it to Demetrius. "I can't raise a glass, so this will have to suffice. Here's to writing."

Demetrius took the flower. "And to writers."

"Yes, writers," Zoey said.

Demetrius turned and walked back toward the sidewalk. As he did, Zoey called after him. "Rus-D?"

"Yes?"

"Anything that gives you joy, don't ever give it up or give up on it."

Demetrius smiled. "Okay."

Chapter 15

DEMETRIUS WAS SITTING in a corner of the living room at the Inn, near a window overlooking the back-yard. The other guests at the Inn were drifting in, sampling the appetizers and having wine, but he sat apart from them, focusing on the view as he reviewed his conversation with Zoey.

Billy Williamson burst through the front door and moved with urgency to Demetrius's side. He was carrying a folded newspaper, and he stretched an arm out so it was directly in Demetrius's line of vision. "Look at this!"

Sources Say Cyanide Killed
Tolland Murder Victim

Tolland – Connecticut State Troopers have concluded that cyanide was the cause of entrepreneur Ike Karas's murder. According to Tolland Town Councilmember Mark Wells, police are questioning residents about recent purchases of products that contain the lethal substance. Wells himself is among those whom the police have investigated, although there is no evidence to suggest that he is a suspect in the murder. No arrests have been made in the recent murder, which took place in Mr. Karas's historic home on Tolland Green. Troop C has not returned calls seeking further information.

The single paragraph was wedged between ads for a tree trimming service and a rug sale.

"Interesting," Demetrius remarked. He looked at the guests who had been chatting with Katherine Conrad; they were all watching him and the officer. "Let's go out into the yard," Demetrius said. And then, to the group: "We don't want to interrupt your conversation; please excuse us."

Outside, the two men sat. "Shultz is gonna kill me," Billy said.

"Nonsense. There's nothing here that's out of line. You did interview Wells, didn't you?"

"I did. That's not the point. The point is, it's in the damn paper. Schultz hates it when the press talks about open cases, and that part about 'no arrests' is going to *really* tick him off. He's gonna go ballistic. He could fire me."

"I assume this is from Virginia Irving. Did you talk to her?"

"Of course not. I'm not an idiot. I can't talk to the press without Schultz's permission, and he never gives anybody permission."

"So, she got it from Wells."

"Who else? It was just the two of us, and what Ginny said is what happened. He's the only other one who knew about it." Billy could not sit still, and his face was flush. He wiped his forehead constantly.

"Billy, calm down. You were working the case. He can't chastise you for doing what he told you to do."

"That's not going to cut it with him. I'm screwed."

"No. You can call Irving and ask her to tell Shultz that you weren't the source for the story."

"You don't understand. He hates her, hates that paper. He won't take her call. She leaves a phone message for him, he'll know it's her number, and he'll delete the message pronto."

Demetrius sat back in his chair. He took a long sip of wine and stared at the fading sky for a moment. Billy fidgeted, tinkering with his badge, brushing imaginary dust off his hat. Demetrius laughed quietly and smiled. Billy saw the smile and leaned forward.

"What?" Billy asked.

"Is there a men's shop in Rockville?"

Billy's frown was deep and dark as he answered. "Yes, there's a place on Hartford pike. They do tuxes for proms and stuff, but they've got regular clothing, too. What's that got to do with anything?"

"I packed casual, so I don't have anything I can wear to a meeting."

"A *meeting*? What meeting?"

"I think it's time you introduced me to Commander Shultz. I'm going to need a blazer."

* * *

Are you telling me this guy, some stranger from LA, is working on *our* murder case?"

"Not exactly," Billy responded. "I heard he was staying at the Inn, and he knows a lot about crime and people who commit crimes. I asked him to kind of look over my shoulder, make sure I'm not missing anything."

"What the hell, Billy?" Shultz turned to Demetrius. "You 'know a lot' eh? How's that work? You retired the uniform—a detective, private eye?"

"No, sir. I'm a novelist. I was a public defender for a year, some years ago."

"Christ. Just what I need to hear. You lost your mind, Williamson?"

"No, sir. Mr. Clarke has been helpful. He had a great idea, got us into Karas's house. We cased the place, searched for clues."

"*We*? *Both* of you? You mean you gave him access to the crime scene?"

"He had some useful insights, sir."

"And compromised the investigation. You have any idea what some hotshot lawyer's gonna do with that, we go to trial?"

Billy coughed but didn't speak. Shultz glared at him before turning to Demetrius and asking, "You the jerk who planted that story in the paper?"

"Absolutely not," Demetrius said. "I've seen the story. It's pretty obvious that Mark Wells is the source."

"Wells? Why would he do that?"

"If I had to guess, I'd bet that Ms. Irving wasn't talking to him about the murder. She covers the Council and other events around town, so it seems likely that she called to ask Wells about something else, and the interview with Billy came up."

"You're telling me you didn't talk to her?"

"I have met her, sir, but I made it clear that I couldn't be a source for her. I made it clear that I can't—I won't—discuss the case with her."

"I'm not buying any of this," Shultz said. "Nobody, and I mean *nobody*, in my shop talks to the press except me. And I don't talk to the press. This story is a direct violation of my command."

"Does Mark Wells work for you?" Demetrius asked as gently as he could, but Shultz didn't mute his anger at all.

"Of course not!"

"Then Wells can't break your rules. There's an easy way to sort this out, of course."

"Yeah? What's that?"

Demetrius turned to Williamson. "Billy, you got a number for Wells?"

"Of course."

"Let's give him a call."

Shultz looked just a little flustered, but it was only momentary. "Hold on, pal," he said. "You don't give orders to my people. You got that?" He turned to Billy. "What the hell were you doing talking to Wells in the first place? You hadn't done that, this damn story never happens, and I don't have to answer to headquarters about a case we aren't solving."

Billy started to speak, but Demetrius held up a hand and beat him to it. "As I understand it, sir, Billy was following your orders."

"The hell you say. What's he talking about, Williamson?"

Billy drew a deep breath. Demetrius caught his eye and winked. Billy carefully recounted Shultz's admonition about finding cyanide purchases, the discovery of Wells's stockpile of weed killer, and his interview with Wells about that purchase. When he was done, Billy said, "It's all in the report I sent to you a couple of days ago, sir."

"See?" Demetrius said. "Your officer acted on your directions, and the first interview he conducted was with somebody who talks to the reporter all the time. You ask me, it's no harm, no foul."

Shultz's eyes were hard, but he didn't speak. He picked up his copy of the paper and looked at the story, then crumpled it into a ball and fired it across the room. "Enough of this," he said. "Billy, no more. You hear? And Mr. Clarke, I want you off the case, out of my hair, gone. That clear enough for you two?"

"Crystal clear," Demetrius said. "But, meaning no offense,

it's not a good idea."

"You got some stones on you, buddy. I suppose you're going to tell me why?"

"If I may. You're up against a wall of indifference. Most of the people in Tolland aren't the slightest bit upset that Karas is dead. They didn't like him, and they wanted him gone. So, he's gone, and nobody much cares who made that happen. Nobody is cooperating with Billy. Nobody's telling him anything that will help him solve the crime because, comes down to it, they don't care if the murderer gets caught."

"Then I'll get one of my senior guys to work on it."

Demetrius shook his head. "That won't matter. They'll give anybody you send in the same cold shoulder Billy's getting. On the other hand, a few of them *have* opened up to *me*. I'm just a guy who used to spend his summers here, a visitor with no axe to grind. Some know Billy and I have been talking the case over, but they're still chatting with me. I think that's because they don't take me seriously. You know, just some goofy writer dipping his toe in the water. Anyhow, if the townspeople talk to me, I can be Billy's eyes and ears. Yours, too.

"And here's what I've learned," Demetrius continued. "Ike Karas fired Janice Young and treated her like dirt. There's no love lost between those two, and Janice's husband thinks killing Karas was a public service. Mrs. Baker, lives across the street, despised Karas, too. And when he hired gunslingers to try to throw Pamela Throop and Mark Wells off the town Council, he made lifelong enemies of each of them. I'll bet you that none of those people would have told Billy about their feelings. They've exposed good motives because I'm just a visitor who loves Tolland as much as they do. They talk to me."

145

Billy cleared his throat. "There's something else, sir."

"What?"

"I know it sounds a little crazy, but Mr. Clarke can think like a killer. He plots, he anticipates, he lives in bad guys' skin, and he thinks like they do. He noticed stuff in Karas's house that I didn't because that's Mr. Clarke's work, his profession. He's all about clues, sir. He knows where to look for them and how to understand them. His instincts are great whether he makes it all up or it's the real thing. At least, that's what I've seen."

Shultz put his elbows on his desk, cradled his chin in his hands, and closed his eyes. Billy and Demetrius waited until he finally spoke. "When I asked Command to send you to me, Williamson, I thought I'd made a smart move—bright young man, top of his class, sharp instincts."

"Thank you."

"Shut up. First major case lands in your lap, you go right off the rails. No progress, no new evidence, you bring some total stranger in who's stomping all over our patch. And now, the damn thing is in the paper, and I'm looking like a sap."

Billy's head drooped.

"And yet," Demetrius said, "he's still bright, still sharp, and we both know he's more than eager to learn. That story in the paper wasn't his fault. Neither is the town's attitude about Ike Karas. If I were you—"

"Which you sure as hell are not."

"All the same, if I were you, I'd give Billy some room, let him lean on me when he needs to and do his job. Look at it this way, sir. If you pull him off the case now, you will be the sap. But if you let him work it, I believe he can sort this thing out. Then, you won't be the sap, you'll be the wise leader who spotted a winner and let him shine."

Shultz rolled his chair back and propped his boots on his desk. He cradled his chin again and sat in silence. The silence broke when he sighed. "Two things," he said. "First, there is no way this dude," he pointed to Demetrius, "shows up anywhere in our paperwork. No name, no mention, no hint that he has anything to do with this case. And sure as hell not in the damn newspaper. You got that, Williamson? Radio silence from here on."

"Yes, sir."

"Two," Shultz continued, "you've got *one* week. Not a minute more."

Billy nodded firmly.

"Nice to meet you," Demetrius said, rising and offering his hand.

"Get out of my office," Shultz said without accepting the hand. "I got work to do." Demetrius and Billy were at the door when Shultz called after them. "Nice blazer, Clarke. You get that on Rodeo Drive?"

"No sir," Demetrius answered. "Went all the way to Rockville for it."

In the parking lot, Billy took his trooper hat off and tossed it on the front seat of his cruiser. He pulled a bandana out of a back pocket and wiped his brow and temples, breathing deeply. "I was sure I was gone," he said.

"Nah. Wasn't going to happen," Demetrius reassured him.

"You saved my tail, that's for sure."

"That's not entirely true, Billy. I can talk to the man in a way you can't because . . . You know Bob Dylan?"

"Sure."

"'If you ain't got nothin', you got nothin' to lose.' Shultz can't touch me, so I can be direct with him. But that's not what saved your job, my friend. *You* did."

147

"How?"

"Shultz told you. He knows you're capable, and he went out of his way to bring you under his wing. That hasn't changed. You're still on the job because, comes down to it, Shultz wants you on the job. You heard him say so."

Billy nodded, feeling more confident. "Roger that," he said. "But you were on my six the whole time, right there. I don't know how to thank you for that."

"No need for thanks, Billy. Let's get together first thing tomorrow and figure out what we're going to do. There's still a murder to solve, remember?"

"Yeah. Listen, I have my rounds to do, but I could swing by the Inn later, around 2 or so. That work?"

"Nope. I'm going to walk across the street and change. Then, I'm going to get a sandwich and a bag of chips and drive down to Crandell's Pond, where I'm going to sit in the sun and swim and maybe read a little. And think. It's a great place to think."

Billy smiled. "Sounds like fun," he said, "except maybe for the reading part. Not my cup of tea."

Demetrius laughed. "Music to a writer's ear, my friend. See you tomorrow."

"First thing. Thanks again."

Demetrius gave Billy a salute and turned, walking toward the Inn. As he strolled along, he took off the blazer and threw it over his shoulder.

Chapter 16

"ANY IDEAS, pal?"

"A couple."

Billy, in uniform, and Demetrius, in khakis and a polo shirt, were walking slowly down the sidewalk along the Green. They both nursed cardboard cups of coffee.

"Shoot," Billy urged.

"First, the Granthams. She was a sort of unofficial spokesperson for the preservationist crowd; she was always the first to address the Council during the Karas hearings. He's an attorney, and Virginia Irving reported that he was donating a ton of free time to fight Karas's army of lawyers. We ought to at least check on them. I assume some of the rude emails Karas sent were to one of them? Or both of them?"

Billy nodded. "He insulted each of them a lot. What else?"

"It dawned on me that we've been looking at one piece of the murder in this case through a keyhole. We need to open the door."

"What part?"

"The muffins. We've been concentrating on the day he ate the muffin, but there were six of them, remember? So, the real question isn't when he ate the muffin, it's when the muffins arrived."

"I don't see that."

"We don't know that the muffins arrived on the day he

149

died. Whoever gave him those muffins opened a window of at least six days—he could have died a week later. He just happened to pick the wrong muffin first. So, the real question is, when did he get the muffins?"

"They could have been delivered a few days before he ate one."

"Exactly. We need to ask around on the Green, see if anybody saw something a week or so before he died. A visitor, a delivery man, a box at the front door, maybe even a delivery to the back deck where he got his morning paper delivered."

"Jimmy Dalton," Billy said. "He might have seen the muffins days earlier, but I didn't ask him about that."

"Now's the time."

"You want to take the Granthams?"

"Sure," Demetrius agreed. "You know where they live?"

"They're near the top of Cider Mill Road, about seven clicks down. Opposite side of the street from Parish house, catty-corner from the Youngs' property line."

"I can find it. You take Jimmy and see if there's anything in that vast network of cop intel on either Grantham. Let's talk this evening, see what we've got."

"Okay."

The men had gotten almost to the old Town Hall when they were halted by a shout. "You two! Get back here." Tenny Baker was standing at the top of her front porch. She was leaning on the porch railing, one arm extended and an index finger pointed directly at them.

"She sounds peeved," Billy noted.

"And she looks it, too."

Both men waved and reversed course.

"Good day, Ms. Baker," Billy greeted her.

Demetrius doffed his driving cap and bowed just a little.

"You two walk past my door without bothering to greet me? Who raised you boys, wolves?" Her tone was gentle, but there was no smile.

"Our apologies," Billy said. "We were too busy talking. Sorry." He tipped his hat.

Tenny moved from the railing to stand in the center of the porch. A harsh grimace crossed her face as she moved, and Demetrius thought her knees buckled just a little. She quickly recovered, but the pain in her eyes remained for a moment.

"It's a pleasure to see you and that beautiful little garden below your porch, ma'am," Demetrius said, taking a step closer. "How are you feeling, Ms. Baker?"

Tenny gave Demetrius a stern glare. "Fine as wine, fit as a fiddle, young man. Never better."

"Good to hear," Demetrius said.

"I've got some apple fritter batter ready to go. Would you two like to sample them for me?"

"I can't," Billy said. "I have work to do. It's sure tempting, but I need to get going."

"Thank you," Demetrius said, "but I have an engagement as well."

"No matter," Tenny replied. "Lucinda's on her way, and she'll eat the whole batch if I let her." As she spoke, a battered sedan with mismatched tires—one of them the smaller temporary spare—pulled to the curb. The door opened, emitting a piercing squeak, and Lucinda climbed out. The orange headset was in place, and she was accompanying Katie Perry. "Remove that thing, young lady," Tenny said, pointing. "Polite ladies do not shun their elders in such a rude fashion."

Lucinda didn't hear Tenny as she was still singing, a little off-key. "You're gonna hear me roar."

Demetrius waved at Lucinda and mimed removing the

headset. She gave him a blank look and then understood, wrapping the earphones around her neck.

"That's better," Tenny said. "Now, a proper greeting, if you will, young lady."

Lucinda laughed. "Good morning, Mrs. Baker. How are you feeling today?"

"Well, thank you. So long as you do not expose me to that dreadful thing and its dreadful music, you're welcome. If I'd known how intrusive that machine is, I never would have given it to you, that's certain."

"Yes, ma'am," Lucinda said. "I know you hate it, but it makes my life so much easier, just like I said it would. You notice I'm five minutes early?"

Tenny checked her watch. "Three minutes, but I take your point. Good for you."

"That's 'cause this phone keeps my calendar for me, and it alerts me when I'm supposed to be someplace. I set the alarm fifteen minutes ahead just to be sure I'm on time, the way you like it. Apple fritters?"

"Mixed, ready to cook," Tenny said.

"Well then," Lucinda said, "let's get going." She waved at the two men and bounded up the porch steps, holding the front door open as Tenny slowly moved through it.

"Let's get moving, too," Billy said cheerfully, "before she thinks of something else we've done wrong."

Demetrius laughed.

* * *

"**M**ay I help you?"

"Denise Grantham?"

"Yes."

"My name is Demetrius Clarke. I once spent summers in

the house just up the street. I'm visiting Tolland, and I'm fascinated by the way it hasn't changed, even though it has. I'm especially curious about the way the Green has been preserved and protected, and when I looked it up in the library, the local paper said you have a lot to do with that. May I have a moment of your time?"

"Were you where the Youngs live? Parish House or that smaller cottage across the street?"

Demetrius smiled. "As far as everyone else is concerned, yes, Parish House."

"What do you mean?"

"It'll always be Church House, or maybe Aunt Beth's house, to me. I didn't know Jeremiah Parish built it until I came back here. Either way, it's a fine old home."

"Yes, it is. Can I offer you some coffee?"

"That would be lovely, thank you."

Denise led Demetrius through the house to the kitchen, poured coffee, and continued to a back door opening onto a stone-on-sand patio.

"When did you live here, Mr. Clarke?"

"Demetrius. Ages ago. I was just a youngster. Aunt Beth sold the place by the time I was thirteen, but I spent my summers here until then. It's still wonderful. I love walking along the Green."

"We all do," Denise said. "Everybody in town understands how special this place is. Well, almost everybody."

"Ike Karas?"

"Exactly. That man had no respect."

"You led the fight against him?"

"Not by myself. There was a sizable group of us. We met frequently during that fight, and everybody contributed."

"But you got quoted a lot in the paper. So did your husband."

"My husband, Will, was a godsend, it's true. Mr. Karas had all these experts, consultants, engineers, lawyers. All of them spoke legalese—gobbledy-gook and hoo-ha. But Will had a way of cutting through that so people could understand what it meant. All I did was talk sense."

"And effectively, as it turned out. You won."

"We were always going to win," Denise said, her eyes glowing. "History, preservation, the law, reverence for the past. We had all that on our side. They had a nasty guy who wanted to crush everything in his way to get what he wanted. It was one of those movies where the good guys just can't lose."

Demetrius caught and held Denise's eyes. "And the bad guy ends up dead."

Denise winced. "Yes. I sincerely hope that has nothing to do with our confrontation. Nobody liked him, but killing him, especially after he lost, that just isn't . . . It just isn't . . ."

"It isn't Tolland?"

"Exactly. We're a small town, after all, so being kind to one another is especially important because everybody knows everybody—there's no place to hide here. But even without that, these are good people who do their best to get along, be friendly. Violence just isn't part of our community."

"Well, it is now, like it or not. Somebody poisoned Ike Karas. It doesn't seem likely that the killer was from someplace else, does it?"

Denise stared into her coffee cup. "No, I'm afraid it doesn't make sense, but I don't like the thought that it was one of our neighbors."

"I understand there's an investigation underway and that nobody knows anything," Demetrius said. "No clues, no suspicions, not even a wild guess. It's an enigma, isn't it? On the one hand, murder just isn't Tolland, and yet, with a murder at hand, Tolland doesn't have anything to say."

"Well, if nobody actually saw anything . . . I mean, how can it be a cover-up if people really don't know what happened in the first place?"

"But that seems just as unlikely, at least to me. Surely, people—even people who really don't know anything about it—have wondered."

Denise nodded.

Demetrius smiled. "All this silence just seems odd to me. Isn't it somehow out of character in this community? Nobody even wants to implicate their most disliked neighbor—you know, some annoying idiot who deserves to be locked up. I imagine, for example, that you—probably you and your husband—must have wondered if so-and-so might have killed Karas."

Denise blushed, blinking furiously as if it would fan her glowing cheeks. She examined her coffee cup anew.

"Forgive me, ma'am. If I'm being too nosy, just say so."

"Denise, please," she said. "'Ma'am' just isn't me. It's true, of course. I'm certain there has been plenty of dinner table guessing. At least, that's where Will and I talked about it."

"And?"

"Will thinks it's one of those consultants Karas used. The word is he refused to pay several of them when he didn't win. So, Will figures somebody from New York snuck into town and killed Ike. I agree with you, though. I'm pretty sure it's somebody here."

"Who?"

"I can't say. I mean, I don't want to throw suspicion on somebody who could be innocent. I don't know anything; it's just a hunch. What good is that?"

"It's better than nothing, Denise. The police have to start

somewhere, don't they? Where would you tell them to look?"

Denise's mouth tightened, and her voice dropped to a whisper. "Mark Wells."

"No kidding."

"He has a temper. He's good at keeping it controlled, but when he can't or won't control it, he's explosive. After one of the Karas hearings, when everything was dragging on, he took Karas aside and roared at him. They were in the hall, outside the hearing room, but we all heard it. Mark sounded completely out of control. Pam Throop finally went out and separated them, but it was ugly until then."

"Did Wells threaten Karas? Did you hear a threat?"

Denise sighed. "Karas shouted that he was prepared to fight the Town Council 'to the death'—those were his words. And Mark said, 'That would be the perfect solution.'"

Demetrius nodded. "Not a direct threat," he said, "but still . . ."

"It's just a guess, like you asked. I don't believe Mark did it, not really. He was just so screaming angry that night, and others tell me he's gone off like that before—I don't know about that, though. But I sure heard *that* one. Mark was furious."

"A brawl in the hall," Demetrius said. "Has a nice lilt to it, don't you think?"

Denise giggled. "A rhyme about crime," she said.

"Touché. Do you bake, Denise?"

"What?"

"Baking: pies, cakes, muffins, that sort of thing."

"I'm afraid not. I don't have the time for it."

"I understand. Fighting off an assault on the Green is probably more important in any event."

"I think so. So is raising a nine-year-old. More coffee?"

"No, thanks. I only stopped by to learn a little more about

how the town saved the Green and how you helped. I must say, I'm impressed with the work you did. I certainly appreciate it, and I don't even live here. Still, I'm sure I've taken enough of your time."

"I'll show you out."

They went to the front door. Demetrius stood on the top step, looking across the street. "Those houses weren't there when I was a kid. That land was vacant. There were a bunch of blueberry plants on it. When I was old enough to need a little money—you know, to buy a model car or put streamers on my bike handles—I'd take a pint basket from our kitchen and pick the berries and sell them to neighbors, usually summer people like us."

"How sweet."

"It was fun, although it turned out to be hard work. Every time I'd fill a basket, I'd take 'em home to wash them before I delivered. Every time I did that, my grandmother would pick over the basket and throw away the berries she said weren't good enough. She said it wasn't right to sell somebody something that wasn't as good as it could be."

"Good for her."

"Yes, I know that now, but I wasn't happy about it back then. I'd have to go back and pick more berries so the basket would be full again. I resented her interference."

"But you learned the lesson."

"That I did."

"Tolland values," Denise said. "A person could do worse."

"At least one person in Tolland has done just that," Demetrius reminded her. "If you think of anything that might help the police find out who, you should give Billy Williamson a call."

"I will," Denise agreed. "But I'm pretty sure I don't know

anything more than I told you."

"You're not alone," Demetrius said. "I enjoyed meeting you. Thanks."

"You're welcome. Enjoy your stay here."

* * *

"**J**immy Dalton didn't see any muffins," Billy informed Demetrius. "He says nobody left them on the deck—he's sure he would have noticed that. He said he never looked at the front of the house; Karas didn't want the paper left there. Jimmy always went straight back on the driveway, never anywhere near the front door. He told me that if he'd seen any muffins, he probably would have swiped one or two."

"An honest lad, then."

"Kind of. What he told me was that Karas was the only person on his paper route who never once tipped him. Didn't even let him keep the change when he paid. Jimmy said if he'd had the chance to snag a couple of muffins, it would have been like getting the tip the guy never gave him."

Demetrius laughed. "Takes a special talent to make a harmless kid hate you."

"Yeah. So, how'd you do at the Grantham place?"

"Denise said she didn't kill him, no surprise there. I didn't get any inkling that she was anything but honest; I'm not sure she'd know how to lie. When I pressed, she said she thinks Mark Wells might be a candidate, but she called that a 'hunch,' and she doesn't have anything to back it up. Just another dead end. Nice house. But nothing. Sorry."

"Me, too. Now what?"

"Not sure. On my way back from the Grantham house, I checked in with Janice Young and Zoey Caldwell. Neither of them saw anybody deliver anything to Karas or his house.

Janice is too far down the street—can't see his place from hers—and I'd forgotten, but Zoey wasn't in town until after Karas was killed. Ran into Lucinda, too, coming out of Ms. Baker's house, and she didn't see anything either."

"Too busy rockin' out to the Stones?"

Demetrius chuckled. "No doubt."

"How about the Walker family?"

"Who are they?"

"House next door to Karas. They're the ones who called us when Jimmy ran over there after he found the body. Mary Walker's on the Council, and I'm pretty sure it was her kids Karas cursed out when they cut through his backyard coming home from school. The husband, Richard, travels a lot—sales, I think. I don't know him except to nod at."

"They're in a perfect position to see a delivery, right next door. You have contact with them?"

"I see Mary at Council meetings. Nice enough lady."

"Give her a call, see if she saw a delivery."

Billy made a note in his pad. "Got it."

"Remind her not to talk to Virginia Irving about the case, right?"

Billy nodded enthusiastically and made another note, grinning broadly.

"I'll drop in on Tenny tomorrow, ask her about a delivery," Demetrius said. "If I run into anybody on the Green, I'll ask them. You do the same. Might be a good idea to drop in on the swap meet, too. Maybe one of the vendors saw something."

"Sure. And Bonnie Bondurant. She's all over this town all the time. She might have seen or heard something."

"Good idea."

The men walked up the Green past the antique shop and the old Tolland jail, beyond the town's primary intersection. It was dusk and quiet, warm, and damp.

A pickup truck came up the street at speed, slowing briefly as it passed Demetrius and Billy. Then, it sped up the street, pulled into a driveway, made a tire-screeching K-turn, and came back down toward the men. The truck's headlights flashed on and off several times as it pulled over and stopped. Mark Wells jumped out of the passenger side, and Danny Dalton exited from behind the wheel.

"You, Williamson!" Dalton shouted. "We been lookin' for you. Wanna talk. Now."

Under his breath, Billy said, "Danny Dalton, Jimmy's dad."

Dalton was scowling deeply, and his arms, in a sleeveless tee shirt, bulged. His fists were clenched. Wells caught up and seemed less menacing but equally intent. As they crossed the road and approached, Billy tipped his hat and said, "Mr. Dalton. Councilman. Good to see you both this evening. Lovely, isn't it?"

"Screw the sweet talk, Williamson," Dalton said. "We got something to say to you." Dalton hung his thumbs in his jeans and stood a few feet from Billy and Demetrius, balancing on his toes.

"Okay. What's up?" Billy asked.

"I told you before, leave my kid out of your chintzy investigation. You want to talk with Jimmy, you come through me. You got that?"

"I ran into him down at the pond," Billy said. "I hoped he might have seen something at Karas's house we didn't ask him about before. He hadn't, so that's that."

"I don't care about any of that. I told you to leave him out, and I meant it." Dalton took a half step forward.

Billy and Demetrius were side by side, but when Dalton

moved, Billy moved forward and to his left, placing himself directly between Dalton and Clarke. Demetrius was impressed with the speed and grace that propelled Billy—he had moved like a dancer—and surprised to see the potent aggressiveness Billy assumed without saying a word. Dalton noticed it, too, and took a step back.

"I apologize, Mr. Dalton," Billy said. "You did ask that we leave Jimmy out of it, and I admit I forgot about that. Still, he was very cooperative. Polite, too. He's a good kid."

"Don't be talkin' to him again without me, y'hear?"

"Roger that, sir." Billy turned to Wells. "Was there something else you guys had in mind?"

"It's about this investigation you're running," Wells said. He spoke with deliberate care, and Demetrius sensed that he was making an effort to control his anger. He couldn't control his demeanor, though; his eyes were flashing, his nostrils flared, and his mouth was snarling.

"The murder? Ike Karas?"

Wells sneered. "What else? Somebody else get murdered?"

"No, sir. Not as far as I know."

"Of course, Karas. I don't suppose you've gotten anywhere?"

"We're still investigating."

"I'm all too aware of that, Billy. You investigated *me*, for crissakes. You're messing with Danny's kid, poking around the Green, checking up on me and the rest of the Council."

"That's how investigations work, Mr. Wells."

"Yeah? Well, investigations are supposed to end, right? You're supposed to figure out who killed that bastard and get 'em into a court room."

"That's the goal."

"But you haven't turned up jack, have you? Nothing."

161

"As I say, we're still—"

"Can it. The whole village is in turmoil, everybody's chattering away about the murder. People are nervous, they're edgy, nobody's sure they can trust anybody. That's my point, Billy. This has to end."

"Before we solve the murder? Are you asking me to just forget that Ike Karas was poisoned in his own backyard? I don't see how I can do that, Mr. Wells."

Wells didn't back down. "Everybody I talk to wants this thing to go away. It's making folks uncomfortable. My wife's going half-crazy making sure the doors and windows are locked. My mother-in-law wants to move out of that piss-ant cottage of hers and sleep in our spare room. The whole town's in turmoil. It's got to stop."

Demetrius leaned around Billy's shoulder. "The fears and mistrust won't go away until everybody knows the killer's been caught, sir," he said. "Stopping the investigation won't make anybody safer. If anything—"

Dalton turned to Wells and asked, "This the writer you been tellin' me about?"

"He's the one."

Dalton turned to face Demetrius. "Who the hell are you, pal? What right you got, wandering all over our town stirring people up?"

Billy said, "He's part of the investigation."

"You can't be serious. A writer? From LA?"

"Yes, sir, but he's also an expert of sorts. Dalton, this is Demet—"

"I know who he is," Dalton interrupted. "Whole damn town knows. How's some hotshot from Hollywood gonna solve this thing? That's just crazy."

Demetrius stepped up to stand next to Billy. "I can assure

you," he said, "that I'm not from Hollywood, but I am a product of Tolland. You gentlemen can complain about the pace of the investigation—it's slow, there's no denying that. But you can't seriously believe that things will get better if Billy and his colleagues just walk away from it."

"Nobody liked Karas," Wells said. "There's not a person in this town who doesn't think we're better off with him gone. Folks are more riled up about your efforts than they are about Karas getting whacked. Think about it, the SOB is gone. Where's the harm in that?"

"Our investigation will continue, sir," Billy responded. "That's what we're paid for. That's what we do."

Dalton turned to face Demetrius. "And *you*? What the hell does some dude from LA care about any of this? You don't even live here."

"Or vote here," Wells added.

"There are two reasons," Demetrius said. "First, Billy understands that he's a good cop who has a lot yet to learn. He asked me to listen and ask questions so the investigation stays on track, and I agreed. If it makes you feel better about that, Billy's commander is fully aware of my role and supports it." Demetrius paused to let that sink in.

"But the most important reason that I care is no different than yours," Demetrius continued. "There's a hole in Tolland's soul, Mr. Wells. This town is going to lose something vital if Karas's killer goes free. Tolland will never be the same if somebody commits murder and nobody cares enough to do something about it. This investigation may be about Ike Karas's murder, but it's really about Tolland.

"I came here to find some peace, to visit the one place I could rely on to be kind, thoughtful, honest, neighborly. Tolland isn't historic just because it's old; its heritage and its principles date back centuries. That sense of community ethics is still here, but it's in peril. Like it or not, silence protects Karas's killer. If the whole town just walks away from a murder, Tolland won't be Tolland anymore. That's why I care, and it's why you do, too. All four of us want to repair the place we love."

Demetrius took a deep breath and closed his eyes for a second. The tension in his shoulders eased, and he took a second breath to slow his pulse. Then, he looked from Wells to Dalton and back again.

Wells nodded, and his shoulders also relaxed. Dalton's contemptuous glare hadn't entirely faded, but he relaxed his arms and rolled his shoulders. "Just want it over," he said. "That's all."

"I agree," Billy said. "Yesterday wouldn't be too soon for me."

Dalton nodded. "Yeah. At least speed this sucker up, eh? Feels like it's gonna snow before you get anywhere."

"Are we done?" Billy asked, stepping back.

"Yeah," Dalton said. "Long as you get that you don't go near my Jimmy."

"You have my word."

Wells and Dalton turned to walk back to the truck. Demetrius called after them. "You know, fellas, you can help!"

Wells turned back. "How?"

"Lots of folks in town are pretending like nothing happened and, even if it did, nobody saw it happen. If you let those folks know that Billy needs their cooperation, Tolland might heal a lot faster. Tell them to help solve the murder."

"I'll see what I can do," Wells said.

Dalton didn't floor it when he drove away. Instead, he motored slowly down the road, slowing still more to give Billy

Williamson a casual salute.

Demetrius said, "Hey, kid. You moved to shield me, didn't you? You were going to take on Dalton."

Billy shrugged. "Thought he might go off on us, and the only thing I could think was, if you got beat up when I was standing right next to you, Shultz would fire me, and he'd be right to do just that. I'm supposed to protect Tolland folk, right?"

"You are, and you just did. I wanted you to know that I noticed. I appreciate it. A lot."

"As I said to those two, it's my job. So, did you notice the same thing I did?"

"Dalton's chest? Guy's got some major-league muscle going on there."

Billy smiled. "No, I'm talking about Wells."

"What about him?"

"Well, I just find it interesting that one of the potential suspects in this case is the same guy who just asked us to back off the investigation."

"Go on."

"Well, we know he had access to cyanide. We know he and Karas were sworn enemies. We know Karas went out of his way to attack Wells, tried to throw him off the Council."

Demetrius nodded. "And we know that Wells has a temper. Denise Grantham said his confrontation with Karas after a hearing was mean, loud, and threatening. Second hand, but why would she lie about that?"

"So, means—he's got access to the poison—and motive, sworn enemies. Seems to me that if we have two out of three, it might make our killer just nervous enough to do something."

"Like try to get you to lay off the investigation."

"Yeah. Just like that."

165

Demetrius let his gaze drift up the street for a moment while he absorbed what he heard. Then, he smiled and extended his hand. "See there, Billy? You're thinking just like a good detective."

Billy colored a little, but he laughed and gave his companion a fist bump.

Chapter 17

D EMETRIUS WOKE AND stretched and wandered over to the window, looking out on Tolland Green. It was very quiet, with little traffic and no breeze. Demetrius stood still, entranced by the lush scene and the delightful sense of calm it provided. The reverie ended when a movement distracted him.

Demetrius saw Doctor Kraskin walking from Tenny Baker's front porch toward his British Racing Green Spitfire. When Kraskin got to his car, he tossed a bag into the passenger seat and then stood, watching Tenny's house for a long moment. He heaved a sigh, sliced himself into the narrow bucket seat, and drove smoothly up the street, turning toward Rockville as he passed by Demetrius's window.

After Demetrius showered and shaved, he went down to the dining room. A group of four women on a Girls' Weekend had stayed at the Inn over the weekend, and their enthusiasm had added a measure of energy. Demetrius hadn't minded, but he was glad they had checked out and left before breakfast. He preferred his mornings not include sustained, peppy, animated banter. Instead, Katherine Conrad and Bonnie Bondurant were at the table, two muffins each on their plates, coffee cups steaming in front of them.

"Good morning, Mr. Clarke," Katherine greeted him. "You remember Bonnie, of course. She showed you Parish House right after you got here. We haven't had time to chat for a while, so I invited her to stop in this morning. I knew the ladies would be gone, and I didn't think you'd mind. We can move into the kitchen if you'd rather not join us."

"That's okay; some company would be welcome."

"Apple pecan and blueberry muffins," Katherine announced. "I whipped up some little omelets. They're in the steamer. The ones on the left have cheddar cheese, there's tomato and basil and onion in the ones on the right. Bacon's in the smaller steamer. Bonnie and I are breaking the rules— we're both having muffins."

"There are rules?"

"Well, we're both always fretting about our weight, and we try to watch what we eat. But we made a pact years ago that when it's just the two of us, there are no food rules."

"Which leaves me free to indulge in stuff I'd never eat otherwise," Bonnie said. "How's your visit going, Mr. Clarke? I had the impression you were here for just a few days, so I'm guessing you're enjoying it here in our little village?"

"It's pleasant to be here. Sometimes it's even more than that. So yes, I'm enjoying my stay here."

"He hasn't even made reservations to fly home yet," Katherine informed Bonnie.

"I don't suppose Billy Williamson has anything to do with that?" Bonnie asked, grinning with the question.

Demetrius smiled back. "If I haven't learned anything else, I know without doubt that the grapevine here is quick. It took Billy less than a day to find me. In fact, I believe my connection with Billy's investigation traces directly back to you, Ms. Bondurant."

Bonnie laughed. "I may have mentioned something to him," she said.

"And it's good that you did," Katherine said. "It's dreadful, somebody killed right here on our Green. Billy needs all the help he can get, and Mr. Clarke has been very generous with his time. Jeff and I appreciate it."

"Everyone does," Bonnie added. "Or at least, everybody I talk to says so. Billy's a good man, and most folks around here are glad that Tolland is his . . . what do you call it?"

"His beat," Demetrius supplied.

"Exactly. New folks who fit right in here, most of us go out of our way to welcome them. Billy's one of them."

"What Tenny calls 'good Tolland folk,'" Demetrius recalled. "I'm glad to hear he's appreciated. I know he's dedicated to this community. He's determined to find out who killed Mr. Karas." Demetrius managed to sneak in the first bite of his breakfast.

"Have you given further consideration to buying here?"

Demetrius raised a hand to indicate his mouth was full, finished the bite, and took a sip of coffee. "As you know, I wasn't considering it when I got here," he said.

Bonnie smiled. "And *now*?"

Demetrius hesitated.

"You know, of course," Bonnie continued, "that sooner or later, Mr. Karas's house will be on the market. It's historic, and he did a lot of work on the interior, so it's historic and modern at the same time. I don't know who's going to get the deed, but once it's out of probate, I can chase it down. It would be a fine investment."

Demetrius shook his head. "If I were interested in buying—purely hypothetical—I seriously doubt I could live in that house."

"Me either," Katherine agreed. "That man was the devil. What if the house is cursed because of him, or maybe because

169

his ghost is still hanging around? I mean, it would be creepy even in the daytime. I can't imagine being in there late at night. In the dark. I mean, that would be so spooky."

"I don't believe in all that," Demetrius said, "but I can't argue with the idea that the place might have an elevated air of menace. Plus, I've seen what Ike did to the interior, and it is not only an affront to the house, it's definitely not my style."

"Jeff says it's horrible in there. I heard Karas wanted to tear out the original staircase and replace it with glass. Well, Lucite or something, but it had to be see-through. He asked Jeff to bid on the job. Jeff told me he would never work for that man, but he was too curious about what he'd done inside, so he agreed to a meeting. Boy, was he out of sorts when he got back."

"Glass staircase?" Bonnie asked, her tone shocked. "What a horrible idea."

"He didn't do it," Demetrius said. "I've been inside, and the original is still there."

"You should have seen Jeff that day," Katherine said. "He was as angry as I've ever seen him. He went out to the shed after lunch, and all I heard all afternoon was pounding, hammering, and some language I can't repeat. We had guests arriving that evening, and I was a bit worried that he might, you know, not be at his best for them. So, I asked him to stay back in our quarters. He said if he never saw another human being, it would be okay with him."

"Hmm." Demetrius frowned.

"There will be other properties, Mr. Clarke," Bonnie assured him. "I don't have anything on the Green right now, but they do come on the market now and then. Plus, of course, there's a whole town around the Green, and I've got a number of very attractive newer homes available. I could give you a tour."

Demetrius smiled and shook his head emphatically. "Nope. I appreciate the offer, but I don't think . . . I'm just not sure about where I'm going these days. It feels like a bad time to make a big decision. But I have your card, Ms. Bondurant. It's on the dresser in my room."

Katherine beamed. "The cherry wood one, right? Do you know we found that right across the street in the antique shop? Jeff was mowing the front yard and saw a pickup truck pull up to the shop, and two guys unloaded a bunch of furniture. That dresser was the last thing they moved, and Jeff stopped his mowing and walked right over there the minute he saw it. He bought it on the spot—didn't ask me, didn't even ask me to check it out. He just told Suzy to mark it sold."

"It's a lovely piece," Demetrius said.

"*Now* it is. You should have seen it when he brought it over here, though. It went straight to the shed, I can tell you. I wasn't going to have that wretched thing in this house. But two, maybe three weeks later, he takes me out to the shed and shows it to me, and I barely recognized it. I thought he was teasing me, but he wasn't. He'd taken that wreck and turned it into, well, you've seen it."

"It is perfectly restored, and the wood is beautiful. The finish is so rich that it almost glows in the dark."

"You'll have to show it to me next time, Katherine," Bonnie insisted. "But for now, I'm afraid I have to be moving along. Hugo DeSica has been transferred, so they're moving, and I need to go see how much dressing it'll need before I can show it. They do have four kids, after all."

Bonnie and Katherine walked to the front door, where they embraced and set a date for their next meeting. While they were at it, Demetrius intently finished his breakfast. He was sitting in the living room with a second cup of coffee when his phone rang. "Good morning," he said, answering it.

"Hi. It's Billy."

"Good morning. What's up?"

"I've been thinking," Billy said. "Be okay if I swing by and pick you up? I gotta drive into Hartford. I wouldn't mind the company, and we can talk."

"Sure," Demetrius agreed. "How soon?"

"I'm out here at the end of the sidewalk."

"That soon, eh? I'll grab my wallet and stuff and be right there."

Billy was in jeans and a Dixie Chicks tee shirt, driving his own car instead of a State Trooper cruiser.

"Off duty?"

"Fifty-fifty. I'm technically off the clock, but there's a case coming up, and the DA's office says they can't find the page where I signed an arrest report. They need me to verify that it's my report and sign it again—in person, so that there's a witness. I'm getting it out of the way today."

"On your day off."

"Shultz says that on our days off, we're not off, we're on standby."

"Aye aye, sir," Demetrius teased.

Billy pulled away from the curb and drove slowly down the Green, veering off onto Merrow Road and then onto the Interstate to Hartford. As he had when he was Rus-D, Demetrius leaned back in his seat and watched Connecticut roll by through the window. And, as when he first arrived in Tolland, he was surprised by the depth of his memories and their conformance with the current reality.

While there was much that was new to Demetrius, and the traffic was considerably heavier, he still recognized a number of motels, most with signs that were now decades old. He also recognized a dairy farm restaurant where he and his family had occasionally stopped for lunch on their way to some adventure; the place's specialty drink was something called a Brown Cow. Demetrius was surprised to see a tobacco farm still in place, although it seemed much smaller to him. When he shifted his gaze from the side window to the windshield, the view made him laugh aloud. "I spy Travelers," he said, pointing.

"What?"

"When I was a kid, we didn't drive to Hartford very often. We'd drive by it on our way to Tolland from DC and again when we drove back home. But otherwise, a trip to Hartford was a special occasion."

"Yeah? So?"

"So, when the car comes up to that rise back there, it's the first time you can see the Traveler's Insurance building tower. In our car, the first person to spot it would say—"

"'I spy Travelers.' Got it."

"There wasn't a prize or anything, but it made the trips a little more fun."

"No prize in this car, either," Billy said. "But I'll tell anybody asks me, you spied it first."

Demetrius chuckled. "I'm good with bragging rights. So . . . tell me why I'm here."

"I'm not seeing one piece of this thing clearly. After you and I talked the other evening, right after Dalton and Wells had their talk with us, I figured Wells should be near the top of the list of suspects. We agreed that he's got a motive and the means, too."

"Bags of weed killer."

"Yup. Only, that's where the problem comes up."

"Why, Billy?"

"Opportunity. The way he told me about being lost in the

173

kitchen, I believed him. It wasn't like, you know, something he made up on the spur of the moment. He was sincere, he was laughing at himself, and he even offered his wife as a witness."

"So, he can't bake."

"I don't think so."

"So, how does the weed killer go from a sack at the ball field to a muffin at Karas's house?"

"That's the question."

"Got an answer?"

"Not exactly," Billy said. He glanced over at Demetrius. "Don't laugh."

"You have my word."

"Okay. What if there's more than one killer?"

Demetrius smiled. "Wells gets the poison, somebody else figures out how to bake it into muffins."

"Any maybe somebody else delivers it. That's plausible, right?"

"Sure. The Orient Express is back."

"Huh?"

"Janice Young had the same idea. Instead of one murderer, there's a group, each as guilty as the other. They plan it, execute it, and they all understand that if one of them talks, they all go down. So, there's a conspiracy of silence. It's one of Agatha Christie's most famous stories."

"How'd they get caught?"

"An eccentric little fellow with superhuman intuitive powers figures it out, and when he confronts the suspects all at once, they collapse."

"Superhuman? Like The Hulk?"

"Not exactly. This guy never misses a detail. He knows what motivates people, he sees clues others miss, and his mind is so perfectly logical that once he puts it together, he's invincible."

Billy grinned. "So, would that be you? Or me?"

Demetrius turned one thumb down. "Based on the status of this case, it's neither of us. But even if Janice was joking when she brought it up, it's not an impossible theory. And there's something else that fits."

"What's that?"

"In the Christie book, the killers were righteous. Their victim had it coming."

"We got that in spades, right? So, should we go back to Wells, try to get him to fess up?"

"With what? To do that, we'd need evidence so persuasive that he'd see no way around it. We're a long way from there."

"What about his wife? I could interview her, let her know we know that Mark bought a truckload of cyanide and had more than enough reason to take Karas down. All he needed was a baker. She'd be the logical choice."

"The chances of that are about as good as Shultz having a sense of humor. They have kids?"

"One, I think."

"Your theory's right: either one of them goes down, they both go down, and their kid's an instant prison orphan. They strike you as the kind of parents would do that?"

Billy was changing lanes, and it took a beat or two before he answered. "No. Mark's a Little League dad, and she's PTA active. I just don't see them doing what we're trying to prove they did. They don't seem like killers."

"Killers wear all sorts of costumes, Billy. Charming, romantic, the All-American family-next-door. Preconceptions aren't good tools for solving mysteries; they usually get you in trouble. Unless we find something else, there's not enough to go hard on Wells. On the other hand, it won't hurt to keep the Orient Express in mind. The more we learn about Karas, the

175

more it becomes clear that just about everybody wanted him dead. Two, three, four of them getting together to make that happen isn't the silliest idea anybody ever had."

"So, I'm not completely off track?"

"Hell, kid, we don't even know where the track is. How can you be lost if you don't know where you're going?"

Billy shot his passenger a look. "Why don't I find that comforting?"

Billy took about half-an-hour to comply with the DA's request. When he was done, the two men climbed back into his car, and he drove to Elizabeth Park. At the entrance, Demetrius asked, "What's this?"

Billy's smile was bright. "This is the oldest rose garden in America," he said. "There's a café here and decent food, but that's not the point. When I'm in Hartford, I always try to work it out so I can visit this place. Walking through the garden, all those rose bushes, it's like spending time in heaven. Let's eat first, okay?"

"Fine with me," Demetrius said. He gazed at his friend for a long minute and then said, "Billy, you're just full of surprises, aren't you?"

"If you say so."

The men ate, then strolled in the garden. Demetrius thought the garden was a bit too formal—too carefully manicured—but he didn't say so, and he was more than happy to let the scents of the place carry him back to the days when his grandmother tended her plants.

Back in the car, the men headed for Tolland. The traffic was a little thicker, so Billy concentrated on his driving while Demetrius drank in the passing scenery. When the pace of the traffic slowed even more, Billy relaxed a bit. "So, can I ask you something?" he said.

"Sure."

"You won't get upset?"

"Why?"

"Might be a touchy subject."

"Ah. Well, dive in, and we'll see."

Billy drew a deep breath. "I hear you got screwed by some Hollywood people. Word is, that's why you came to Tolland. To escape. That right?"

Demetrius shifted his gaze and looked directly at Billy. "You heard that, did you? Well, if it's gotten all the way to you, it's a safe bet the whole damn town knows about it."

"Word does travel. Carol, who's the young lady I spend some time with, shares an apartment with a roomie, and the roomie's boyfriend is an intern over at the local paper, *The Journal Inquirer.*"

"Got it. Virginia Irving, then the world."

"I figured, but I didn't ask. It *is* true?"

"Yes. Irving didn't have it quite right, but I had a deal with a production company, and it turned into a nightmare. I had to walk away from it. It wasn't a pleasant experience, and it shook me up some—left me wondering about my future."

"Came back to Tolland to figure it out."

"That was the plan. You asked for my help, and things went a little haywire, but it's still on my mind. Still not sure what I'm going to do. I feel, I don't know . . . off balance, I guess."

"Can I ask you something else?"

"In for a penny, in for a pound. Go ahead."

"The way I heard it, you walked away with a pretty hefty chunk of money. They paid you?"

"Yes. They bought the film rights to a book I wrote. I was supposed to work with them on the production, but I couldn't live with what they were doing to the book, so I quit."

"But they paid you."

"They did."

"Stop me if I'm stepping on toes here, but I'm having some trouble making sense of this."

"How?"

"Well, first, you wrote a book. And somebody printed it, right?"

"I'm published, yes."

"More than one?"

"Four."

"Impressive. And somebody thought one of them was so good that it should be a movie."

"A series, actually."

"For which they paid you."

"Yes, we've certainly established that. Where is this going, Billy?"

"Not quite there yet. You didn't like what they did to your book."

"Hated it, Billy. I hated it."

"You hated what they did to your book, so you walked away."

"That's it in a nutshell. Debilitating and damn frustrating."

The traffic slowed to a crawl, and Billy turned to face Demetrius directly. "*What the hell's wrong with you?!*"

"What?"

"You're good enough to get books published. One of them was so good that it got sold to Hollywood, and they paid you . . . handsomely?"

"It's what my folks would have called a 'tidy sum,' but they meant big bucks when they said it."

"So, you're a successful author, and there are some bozos

in Hollywood who gave you a tidy sum. They were lousy people, but you're free of them. And you pitch a bitch? Me, I'd be celebrating and thinking about what I'm gonna do with all those big bucks."

The traffic picked up, and Billy turned away to concentrate on it. Demetrius stared out the window as they drove along, saying nothing. As they slowed to exit the Interstate and head into Tolland, Billy spoke again. "I didn't mean to upset you," he said.

Demetrius smiled and swiveled to face Billy. "You didn't upset me," he said. "You saw something I didn't."

"What's that?"

"A fresh perspective."

Billy smiled. "Yeah? Cool."

They crossed the overpass. Demetrius looked past Billy and saw a sign: *Tolland Family Restaurant and Pizza.* "You hungry, Billy?"

"A little early, but I could handle dinner."

"Pull over," Demetrius said. "Pizza's on me."

Chapter 18

BILLY DROPPED DEMETRIUS at the Inn. Katherine Conrad met Demetrius at the door. "Good evening, Mr. Clarke. Jeff and I were just about to have supper in the kitchen. It's chicken with pasta and a salad. I didn't make a dessert, but we can scrounge something up. Jeff said I should invite you to join us."

"I just ate with Billy, so I'll have to decline. But please tell Jeff I'm flattered."

"You should be. There aren't a lot of people Jeff cares to talk with. You could join us anyhow, have a glass of wine. Or, Jeff has a collection of beers; he orders them online. When he sees a label he likes, he orders a six-pack. I don't drink beer, so I can't recommend anything, but Jeff sure can. I don't quite understand where this came from, this beer thing. Jeff didn't ever drink beer until a year or so ago. Funny, isn't it? You think you know somebody really well, and then they do something completely unusual."

Demetrius nodded emphatically. "Elizabeth Park."

"What?"

"I just had a similar experience. Somebody I thought I knew surprised me, too. Twice, actually. Thanks again for the invitation. Perhaps we can have supper together another time. Right now, though, I've got a lot on my mind, and I'd liked to take a walk around the Green. So, I'm going to run up and change into my sneakers. Enjoy your supper."

"Okay."

When Demetrius came back downstairs and headed for the front door, he was startled to see Jeff Conrad waiting for him. Jeff was holding a flashlight. "Streetlights on the Green are poor, sidewalks buckled some," Jeff said. "Don't want you trippin' or gettin' hit by a ca'. Take this."

Amused and touched, Demetrius took the flashlight and clapped Jeff on the shoulder. "Thanks, Jeff. Very thoughtful."

"Nothin'."

Demetrius walked the length of the Green. He spent a moment gazing down the hill at Parish House—several windows glowed with lights. Then, he crossed the street. On a whim, he walked up to the front door of the old Town Hall. It was locked, and Demetrius felt a twinge of disappointment. He had hoped to discover that it was as he remembered it when he'd been taken to meetings once or twice: a large meeting space, somber like a chapel until it transformed with the energetic din of a campaign rally or a spirited debate. Demetrius returned to the sidewalk and walked briskly, feeling agitated.

When Demetrius arrived at the front of the antique store, he wasn't satisfied, so he turned and retraced his route in reverse. By the time he reached the steps at the Inn, he was feeling a little tired but no less unsettled. He left the flashlight on the registration desk and went up to his room.

Lying on the bed with the lights out, Demetrius tried to settle and sleep. Between Billy's probe of his recent misadventure and the jumbled confusion of the Karas murder, he could not remain still, let alone doze. In his mind, he built a list of suspects.

Meryl and Janice Young both had ready access to cyanide and reasons to hate Karas, as did Mark Wells. Pamela Throop wasn't on the cyanide list, but she shared a strong motive with Wells. Karas had launched personal attacks on Denise and Will Grantham, and they, in turn, had strong connections to Tolland's preservationist cohort, all of whom despised Karas. Danny Dalton hadn't been investigated, but he clearly had a temper, and he and Mark Wells were allies. Other than the chance that she would get a sales commission when Karas's house came back on the market, Bonnie Bondurant seemed an unlikely candidate; she might be the only person in Tolland who had dealt with Karas and come away unscathed. But she was a relentless businesswoman—hungry enough to kill for a commission?

The Walkers, whose children Karas had aggressively berated—could they be tiger parents, intent on removing an abusive next-door neighbor? Reluctantly, Demetrius added Jeff Conrad. Katherine's description of Jeff's fury at Karas's disrespect for his grand old house suggested a motive, and Demetrius was confident that, were he to look, there would be rat poison or weed killer in Jeff's shed. When Demetrius folded in the potential of a group conspiracy and the theoretical possibility that one of Karas's many out-of-town enemies had killed him, Demetrius all but vibrated in frustration. He forced himself to change directions.

Demetrius let his mind drift, considering random facts and fancies. They still hadn't found Karas's cell phone. Why? Only one of the muffins had poison in it, why not the others? Billy Williamson's suggestion of Mrs. Wells as a co-conspirator danced in front of him—"All he needed was a baker." That triggered a new question: home-baked or commercial? And that led to yet another: weed killer or rodent poison?

Demetrius leaned over and grabbed a pen to make a note: "*Sources?*" An image of Lucinda's bright orange headset zipped by, followed quickly by Abby Young's wish to be a "suspit," Tenny Baker's exhausted nap on her porch, and Virginia Irving's absolute lack of information about the murder (the product of a town that just wasn't saying anything). Was their absolute silence by choice or by chance?

Frustrated that he was unable to shut down the torrent of murder miscellany, Demetrius rose and paced the room. He deliberately shifted his thoughts to his conversation with Billy. As soon as Billy had pointed it out, Demetrius understood that his view of the book-to-screen fiasco was so infused with anger that he had lost his way. Billy had seen what Demetrius could not or would not: Demetrius Clarke was a successful, albeit only moderately marketable, writer. He'd made a lot of money when he sold his rights, and while the insults to his work were still real and raw, he had left that ugliness behind.

Demetrius conjured up Billy's "What the hell is wrong with you?" And then another Tolland voice chimed in. Zoey Caldwell had said, "Anything that gives you joy, don't ever give it up or give up on it."

"She's right," Demetrius noted quietly. "And so is Billy." He went to the chair by the window, switched on the table lamp, and picked up his book. He was six pages further along when his eyes began to droop. He carried the book to bed and, two paragraphs later, fell asleep.

* * *

The table lamp next to Demetrius's bed at the Inn was still on when he awoke in the morning. He called Billy about the questions involving sources, and a short time later, Billy parked in the lot next to Crandell's Pond and called Hartford. "Lab. This is Rex," the voice on the other end of the line answered. "How can I help you?"

"Hey, Rex, it's Billy Williamson, over in Tolland."

"Billy. Sup?"

"I need to check a couple of things on the Karas murder. You got a minute?"

There was a pause before Rex said, "Just one."

"Cool. So, I need to know if the muffins we bagged as evidence are homemade or commercial. We don't know the source."

"That it?"

"No, one more—another source question. Can you guys determine what kind of cyanide killed him? I mean, was it rat poison or weed killer? It would help my investigation if I could narrow that down."

Another pause. Then, "Not sure how to tell you this, Billy, but . . . There are protocols here. We all gotta follow them."

"Of course," Billy acknowledged. "If it takes a couple of days to get me the answer, I understand."

"Um, the thing is that priorities govern what we do around here and when we do it. It's the rules. You must understand that . . ."

"Rex, what's going on?"

"Aw, hell, Billy. Here's the deal. We're supposed to focus on live, current cases, and your case doesn't seem to be going anywhere, y'know? You're way down on the list."

"I'm working on a *murder*, Rex."

"Yeah, but you gotta admit that there's not much happening. And we got plenty of other stuff backed up here, hot cases. Word from the bosses is you're not a high priority."

Billy winced. "How long, Rex?"

"Couple of weeks, maybe longer."

"Rex, what the— I don't get this. This case is hot. It's only two weeks old, give or take. I don't agree that it's cold. And

I'm working it hard. I need some help, but you're telling me you can't help because it's not moving fast enough? And then you tell me you're going to slow-walk the help I need, which, the way I see it, makes the case even slower and colder. That make sense to you?"

"What makes sense to me is that if I don't do what they want, I won't have a job. And what they want right now—and I mean right this damn minute—is an analysis of a suitcase full of what appears to be uncut cocaine."

"Great."

"You want my advice, Billy? Get yourself a viable suspect and get us a sample of the stuff you think they used to poison your vic. We can match your sample to the stuff that killed your vic in a hot minute."

"That would be a whole lot easier, Rex, if I know exactly what stuff I'm looking for."

"Probably so, buddy, but I can't help you with that. Gotta go." Rex hung up.

Billy dialed Demetrius's cell phone. "You free for lunch?" he asked.

"Sure. I snagged one of Katherine's corn muffins earlier, but it's all I've had. I could eat."

"I need to sift through the whole damn thing."

"Good idea," Demetrius said. "I spent an hour or more doing that last night. I don't suppose there's a decent deli around here?"

"Over t'Vernon there is. I'll pick you up around 12:30."

"Good."

Ten minutes later, Lucinda rapped on the door of Demetrius's room and opened it. "Housekeeping," she announced.

"Hi, Lucinda," Demetrius greeted her. "Come on in."

The headset came off, and Lucinda nodded a greeting.

"You're still here," she said.

Demetrius smiled. "Having too much fun. No reason to leave."

"Works for me," Lucinda said. "Days when the place is empty are days I don't work. I don't work, I don't get paid, and that's not cool—not cool at all. As long as you're around, at least I get paid for more than just weekends."

"Glad to be of service," Demetrius said. "Things a little tight, I gather."

Lucinda shrugged. "I clean houses. Eddie—he's my boy-friend—does framing and wallboard. We get by. Not rich, and we ain't goin' on a cruise or anything like that, but we got an okay little apartment, beer in the fridge."

"And you get to be in Tolland. Lovely place, good people."

Lucinda shrugged again. "Good as any, I guess."

"I just had a thought. Can I ask you a question?"

"Shoot."

"Did you by any chance clean for Mr. Karas?"

"Fifteen minutes," Lucinda answered. Her reply was tinged with anger.

"How could that—"

"He booked me for what he called a 'beta test,' whatever the hell that is. I show up, and the place is a total nightmare. Walls torn out, he's got guys ripping up carpet, downstairs wall by the backyard is completely gone, and there are guys putting in huge glass doors. I mean, there was dust and grit and carpet scraps and lint, some broken glass, too, all over the damn place."

"And?"

"He looks at me and says, 'Get to work.' I'm like, 'You gotta be kiddin' me.' He says no, he wants me to clean up after these guys every day until they're done. I'm all 'this is way more than I do for everybody else 'round here.' Then, get this, he tells me he's only gonna pay me for two hours, says that's all it should take. I'm like, 'it's gonna take me that long just to get all this carpet crap outta here.'" Lucinda grew more agitated as she talked.

"So, it only took fifteen minutes before you walked out on him?"

Lucinda nodded.

"Good for you!"

"Two hours. Really? Gimme a crew of three, four, and we might get half the downstairs clean. I mean . . . *two* hours?!"

"Definitely out of bounds," Demetrius agreed. "I know you do for Mrs. Baker. Do you have a lot of other clients?"

"Not as many as I'd like, but I keep busy. I do Ms. Caldwell's cottage, but she's hardly a regular. She calls me a couple days before she's comin' to town, and I go in and clean it up for her, but then she does for herself until she goes back to the city. I do the Throops' once a month and the Granthams' place every other week, but Ms. Grantham likes to help, so I don't make quite as much. Then, I got two down past the pond, in that development. They're every week 'cause they got kids, and, you know . . . *kids*." Lucinda gave an exaggerated shrug. "Whaddya-gonna-do?"

"You cover a lot of ground, see a lot of folks. Who do you think killed Ike Karas?"

Lucinda met Demetrius's gaze. "Dunno. Or care."

"Didn't think so. Nice chatting with you, Lucinda. Let me collect my book, and I'll get out of your way."

Lucinda plugged the vacuum cleaner in and left it the in the middle of the room, picked up a bucket, and went into the small bathroom.

Demetrius moved to the door and turned back. "Thanks."

"Sure."

Demetrius walked halfway down the hall before he turned and came back. "Lucinda?"

"Yeah?"

"Could you hand me what's left of that muffin, please?"

"Okay," Lucinda said. She wrapped it in its napkin and handed it over. Then, as Demetrius moved back down the hall, she called after him. "T'woulda been gone when you got back!"

Demetrius went out the front door and stood, watching the Green. He had coffee in one hand and the muffin in the other. Suzy Henderson opened the door to the antique store and stepped out. She saw Demetrius and waved. He toasted her with his coffee mug, then turned and saw a small group of children and three moms on their way into the library. Each of the kids was carrying books. A modest breeze ruffled through the leaves on the trees on the Green. Demetrius took several deep breaths, seeking to draw in the tranquility of the scene before him. After several breaths, it seemed to work, and he took a seat on the steps, content to linger and savor.

A few minutes later, Katherine Conrad opened the Inn's front door and called to Demetrius. "Lucinda's all done up there," she said. "The room is yours again."

Demetrius turned and nodded, hoping that—as entertaining as he had come to view her extended conversations and explanations—Katherine would leave it at that. When she did, he felt a pang of guilt for not having engaged her. "Life's weird," he said to himself.

* * *

Billy ordered a stack of French toast and a side of bacon. Demetrius took a chance on the pastrami and was rewarded.

"That's got to be from Manhattan," he said.

"Wouldn't surprise me," Billy replied. "It's not that far, you know."

"A lot closer than LA."

"You like it there? You missing it?"

"There are many things to like about the city," Demetrius said. "Strong arts support that goes well beyond the movie and TV stuff, a wonderful blend of ethnicity, lively politics, and more. It's got a lot of energy and style, and I've got a good circle of friends there, too."

"Yes, but I hear that the traffic—"

"It's worse than you hear. Everybody drives, and it's so crowded that everything is slow, so the air never gets entirely clean. It's a whole lot better than it used to be, but the perfect weather everybody talks about still has soot in it."

"Don't think I'd like it," Billy said.

"It's a definite negative. But getting away from it helps bring living there into focus. It's hard work getting around in that town, and most things are so far-flung that walking hardly ever makes sense."

"And you breathe all that junk when you do."

"True."

"I think I'll stay right here. Tolland's a good place." Billy raised an eyebrow and gave Demetrius an intensely hopeful look.

Demetrius laughed. "You working for Bonnie, Billy? Drumming up business for her?"

"Nah. Just thinkin' how much you like it here, is all. You could do worse."

"I could indeed," Demetrius agreed. "In fact, I'd give it serious consideration, but I hear there's a murderer on the loose. Doesn't sound like a law and order kinda place."

Billy aimed a finger gun at his friend's forehead. "We shoot folks who talk trash about our village."

"That thing loaded?"

"Nah. If it were, I'd point it at my own head." There was an air of despair in Billy's tone.

Demetrius set his sandwich down. "Something eating you?"

Billy looked up, and Demetrius saw discouragement in his eyes. "I'm not sure I can hack this, Demetrius."

"The case?"

Billy nodded. "I'm completely lost, and it turns out everybody knows it."

"What makes you say that?"

Billy related his exchange with the lab. His tone was unhappy and tense. "I got no doubt Shultz is planning to pull me off and turn it over to somebody else. Sounded to me like he's already told the brass I'm on the way out. I don't want that; you know I don't. But honestly, I can't argue with Shultz about it. All I've done is spin wheels ever since Karas bought it. It took me two weeks to realize I should inquire about the source of the muffins and cyanide, and I didn't even come up with that idea—you did."

"You're not the only one spinning his wheels," Demetrius said. "I haven't been much help."

"You're showing me how to think about murder," Billy pointed out. "That's something."

"But Shultz is all about results. Technique and analysis are fine for novels, but they don't mean a thing in your world if they don't generate an arrest and a conviction. I think you're right about the lab; its protocols seem counterproductive. That's just an impediment you'll have to overcome."

"And I'd love to do just that, but Rex, the lab guy, needs

something solid before I get any help from him. And I don't have any idea where to find something solid. I'm screwed."

Demetrius took a sizable bite of his sandwich and chewed slowly, his focus on a space above and behind their booth. "We can't quit, Billy. *You* can't quit. Let's step back and come at it from a different direction. How about this? Who's the least likely person to have killed Ike Karas? Who can you say with certainty did not do it?"

Billy didn't hesitate. "The kid, Jimmy Dalton."

Demetrius nodded. "Nor Abby Young."

"Nor Carol Porter."

"Who the hell is Carol Porter?"

"Think I've mentioned her, the gal I date. Sweet, teaches fifth grade at the school, has a place in Stafford Springs. She's the one who heard about your Hollywood mess, but she doesn't know Karas from Adam, and take my word, she can't cook worth a damn. If she can bake muffins, I can fly."

"That's cheating 'cause she's not a suspect in the first place."

"Ginny Irving, then."

"Why?"

Billy smiled. "First, 'cause if she did it, I don't think she could resist putting her story on the front page in that damn paper. Second, I don't think she has a motive. Karas took potshots at everybody in town, but I didn't find anything complaining about her—no nasty emails, no letters to her boss complaining about her, nothing—when I went through his desk and searched his computer. He never went after her."

Demetrius nodded. "When I read the coverage of the hearings about his plans for the house, it seemed clear to me that Virginia gave him plenty of room to explain his side even if everybody else didn't support him. The coverage was fair, so he had no beef with her. I accept it; she's off the list."

Billy said, "You pick one."

"Well, Zoey Caldwell. But that's not fair since she wasn't in town until after Karas was killed. So, I'd probably cross off Denise Grantham."

"Because?"

Demetrius thought about it for a second. "Too nice, for one thing. But mostly because she's so devoted to her cause. She wants to protect and preserve Tolland. That's what she lives for, and she's smart enough to know that killing somebody would do real damage to that effort. I don't think she's capable of sabotaging the work she loves."

Billy nodded his understanding. "What about her husband?"

Demetrius shook his head. "I didn't meet him, don't know anything about him other than what I read in the paper. Can't cross him off, but I don't have any reason to suspect him, either."

"Strike Denise, leave Will."

"Do you know him?"

"I'd know him when I see him, I think. But no, not really."

"Who's next?"

Billy picked up a strip of bacon, dipped it in a little pool of syrup, and bit off a couple of inches. As he chewed, his face grew troubled. "Anybody. Everybody. No offense, but this isn't getting us anywhere."

"I'm just trying to find a new way to look at the thing."

"'Preciate that, but it's just so damn frustrating. It's enough to make me sick."

Demetrius leaned back against the booth cushion and regarded his companion. Billy's face was drawn, his color off, his shoulders slumped—he looked like a man who was well and truly sick at heart. "Lunch is on me," Demetrius said.

Chapter 19

DEMETRIUS LEFT THE Inn as the sun was setting and walked all the way down the Green, taking Merrow Road past Parish House and continuing along the road until he got to the pizza shop. He ordered pasta and wine and slowly ate. He ignored the few others in the room and concentrated on the case. His pasta was almost cold when he thought about Billy's despondent tale of the lab and its protocols. He wondered what might have resulted had the lab been willing to determine the source of the muffins or even the cyanide, and an idea burst upon him with such clarity that he jumped up and tossed his napkin on the table. He paid his bill and walked briskly back to the Inn.

Back in his room, Demetrius went to his laptop and fired it up. He conducted a search and found what he sought. He settled in and read several articles slowly and carefully. When he was done, he shut the machine down and leaned back in his chair. "I'll be damned," he said. "Who knew?"

Demetrius grabbed a pad of paper and a pen. When he was done, he had drawn a rough chart with boxes and notes and arrows leading to and fro. The process, the same one he used when he began plotting out a mystery, felt comfortable and easy. When he was done, he sat back and surveyed his work, a clear map of random actions and people, some connected, some not. Combined with the research he'd just completed, the chart made some things much clearer. At the same time, it also brought into sharp focus critical questions that had yet to be asked.

Demetrius picked up his phone and dialed. As he expected, there was no answer. He waited for the beep. "Billy, Demetrius here. Call me first thing tomorrow."

After climbing into bed, Demetrius switched on the bedside lamp and read until he was half asleep. Then, he switched the light off, smiled, and slept until Billy called him at 6:50 a.m. Demetrius was already up, seated at the window, looking over his notes and boxes and arrows as he watched the Green wake up. "Can you get over here around 9:30?" he asked.

"The Inn?"

"Yes."

"I can do that. What's up?"

"We have work to do."

A couple and their daughter were staying at the Inn. They were on a tour of campuses, UConn at Storrs among them. All three were at the table when Demetrius came down, and they chatted as they ate breakfast. The meal included a large bowl filled with a potpourri of local berries, ripe and flavorful. When Katherine joined them, she spent fifteen minutes talking about where all the varieties had come from—who raised them, where they grew, where she had bought them, what they cost—berry by berry. The three adults listened politely. The teenager lasted barely a minute before she started surfing her phone.

When Demetrius was done eating breakfast, he filled his coffee mug and went out the front door. He crossed the yard in the direction of the parking lot and leaned against a tree, sipping and thinking. When Lucinda's battered Honda pulled into the lot and she climbed out, he watched as she fiddled with her phone and put her headset in place. "Here we go," Demetrius said to himself.

Demetrius and Lucinda exchanged greetings, and Lucinda went in. Demetrius resumed his tree-lounging until the State Trooper cruiser pulled into the lot. As Billy exited, Demetrius walked toward him.

"Let's stroll up that way," Demetrius suggested, pointing to the upper portion of the Green.

"You gonna tell me what's going on? Otherwise, I got stuff to do."

Demetrius chuckled. "Walk with me, Billy. If I'm right, it's time to start solving this case."

Billy stared at Demetrius and then turned and started walking briskly up the Green. "You comin' or what?"

Demetrius fell in step. "Lucinda, the cleaning lady, works at the Inn. She's there now."

"So what?"

"I think you should interview her."

"Why?"

"Because I think she knows something important."

"About the Karas case?"

"Yes." Demetrius paused and then turned back toward the Inn. Billy, looking confused, followed. "She has three rooms to do," Demetrius continued. "Mine, a couple in one room, their daughter in another. Lucinda should be there for an hour, maybe ninety minutes."

"Okay. Are you telling me *she* killed Ike Karas?"

"No, I don't think so. But she's connected to it."

"How?"

"It'll be clear soon enough. For now, there are a few questions you need to ask her."

"About what?" Billy asked. Demetrius explained, and Billy listened intently. "You know that sounds a little nuts, Demetrius, don't you?"

"I do, but if I'm right—and I think I am—it's a vital piece of information."

"And you? What are you up to while I'm asking a cleaning lady questions that don't make a whole lot of sense to me?"

Demetrius smiled. "I'm going to convince somebody to do something very, very wrong."

Billy stopped walking and turned, looking completely bewildered.

"Just trust me, Billy. Think of it as a fair trade."

"Huh?"

"Couple of days ago, you showed me how to solve a problem. I'm just trying to pay you back."

Billy tilted his head to one side, still perplexed.

"Look at it this way, Billy. What have you got to lose?"

Billy, sermon somber, looked directly at Demetrius. "My job," he answered.

"Nope. We're not going to let that happen. C'mon, let's get going. You don't want to miss Lucinda, and I'm off to find the person I'm intent on leading astray. We'll talk early this afternoon, compare notes."

* * *

Katherine Conrad led Billy to the landing on the second floor of the Inn. "Lucinda?" she called out. "Can you come to the hall for a second, please?" There was no response. "Lucinda? Out here, please." There was still no response.

Billy moved to stand beside Katherine. "She can't hear you."

Katherine seemed confused. "She can't? Why ever not?"

"No doubt she's got her headset on, and it's probably cranked up."

"Oh."

Katherine walked down the hall to a room with its door wide open. She went in and came back out. Lucinda stood behind Katherine, and Billy thought, *You're going to hide from me? Really?* But before he could speak, Lucinda stepped out and walked down the hall toward him.

"Use that room," Katherine said, pointing to it. "Nobody's in it, so you won't be interrupted."

"Thanks," Billy said. He opened the door and held it for Lucinda. When she moved past him, she gave him a look that was equal parts fear and contempt. "Relax," Billy reassured her. "You haven't done anything wrong. I just need to ask you a couple of questions. That's all."

Lucinda nodded and walked into the room.

* * *

Robert Kraskin's office in Rockville was on the second floor of a generic low-rise medical complex within walking distance of a hospital. The waiting room was appointed with cookie-cutter furniture, including the obligatory coffee table strewn with old magazines. After Demetrius checked in with the receptionist—"No, I don't have an appointment, just a quick consultation, and yes, I can wait"—he took a seat in a chair.

Demetrius was pleased to find that more than half the magazines on the table were automotive—*Car & Driver* and *Road & Track*—most of them with the doctor's home address sticker on them. The elderly woman who was waiting when Demetrius arrived was ushered in, and Demetrius spent his wait scanning the collection.

"Mr. Clarke, the doctor will see you now." The nurse led him down a hall to an examining room and held the door open for him. Demetrius looked in but remained in the hall. A little impatiently, the nurse said, "There's a gown on the examining table. Strip down to your shorts and put on the gown. Doctor will be with you shortly."

"Does he have an office?"

"Yes, but—"

"This isn't exactly a medical visit. No exam involved. Can you show me to his office, please?"

The nurse frowned but then walked him to the last door down the hall. "Mr. Clarke is here, Doctor."

Kraskin looked up from his desk and smiled. "I thought it was you," he said. "The nurse gave me the name, and I was pretty sure I recognized it. Thanks, Cindy."

The nurse gave Demetrius a look of disapproval and closed the door quite firmly when she left.

"How can I help you?" Kraskin asked. "Common cold? Got a bug you picked up at the pond? Broken bone?"

"None of the above," Demetrius answered. "I have to ask you a delicate question."

"Ah, something involving your love life? This is a family practice, so we include that. Otherwise, how would we have families?"

Demetrius laughed. "No. It's more along the lines of the oath you took."

"Hippocrates?"

"Indeed. I want you to tell me something about someone I believe you've been treating."

Kraskin pulled his glasses off and let them drop. They dangled at his chest on a braided leather strap around his neck. "I can't discuss my patients. Ever. Never mind the oath; the federal bureaucracy, HIPAA, says I'd be committing a crime."

"I'm aware of that, and under ordinary circumstances, I wouldn't bother to ask. But this is . . . This is an extraordinary circumstance."

"Don't care. I do find the paperwork we're forced to do now to be burdensome, and if you believe billing Medicare or Medicaid is simple or fast, you're dead wrong. But the privacy protections are important. I not only agree with them, I'm a stickler about it. I'm sorry if I've wasted your time, but I just can't help you."

"I promise you that what I seek will be held in strictest confidence, and once you hear why I need your help, I think you will agree that an exception is warranted. Your waiting room is empty, so will you at least give me a few minutes to explain?"

Kraskin drummed his fingers on his desk for a moment, then folded his hands and sat up. "Go ahead. You're not going to get anywhere, but I've got some time, and you seem quite determined. So, let's give it a shot." He grinned. "Pun intended."

Demetrius gave an appreciative smile and adjusted his position so his eyes were at the same level as the doctor's. Methodically and without any hesitation, he laid out the reasons for his visit and the specific information he sought.

* * *

"Somebody spray-painted the equipment shed over at Cross Farms," Billy informed Demetrius. "Bunch of what my mom calls 'dirty words.' Probably the same morons who were shooting off fireworks over there; teens with too much time on their hands. Anyhow, I have to go over there and talk to the staff, take a look. I got a couple of minutes, but then I gotta scoot."

"Would you rather postpone?" Demetrius asked. "You can go now, and we can grab dinner later, take our time."

"Nope. I want to play back my conversation with Lucinda while it's still fresh. And I've been trying to figure out what you're up to all morning—pretty much spoiled my lunch, too.

So, I'm not about to let that go. Where were you?"

"You first."

Billy checked his watch. "Short version, you were right about her phone, but it's a dead end. Since it was used, she and her boyfriend pulled out both of those little chip cards—the SIM card and the SD. Replaced 'em and threw the old ones away, so the only info in the phone is Lucinda's: her messages, her email, her music. Now, where did *you* go?"

Billy's phone rang, and he punched it. "Williamson," he answered. Then, he paused and listened, nodding. "I understand. Okay, I'm on my way." He hung up and then said to Demetrius, "Damn. The director over at the rec center says she's got to leave within the hour, and she wants to show me what happened and talk to me before she leaves. She's pretty upset. I gotta go."

"We wouldn't want you painting over a crime, Billy," Demetrius teased.

"Cute. So, I guess dinner will have to do."

"Yup."

"Can you at least—"

"Robert Kraskin. I visited the doctor."

"What for?"

Demetrius smiled, then answered. "Just yesterday, you said this case is 'enough to make you sick.' I got to thinking about that, so I went to see a doctor. Pick me up when your shift ends, and we'll go over everything."

Billy drove away, and Demetrius went upstairs. He changed into his swimming suit and a tee shirt and grabbed his hat, his book, and a couple of towels. He walked to the pond, found a relatively quiet spot close to a stand of trees next to the beach, and spent the afternoon reading, dozing, and pondering.

Pamela Throop and her children were at the pond, too. The

kids were playing with a group of peers in the shallows of the pond, tossing a ball and diving after it with abandon. Pamela alternated between monitoring them and skimming a few magazines strewn around her blanket. When the kids came out of the water to forage in a bag of snacks, Pamela asked them to stay out of the water until she returned and walked over to Demetrius. "Good afternoon," she greeted him.

"It certainly is," Demetrius said. "It's just lovely here, bright and sunny and not too hot."

"And no humidity to speak of," Pamela added. "I don't like muggy very much."

"I don't believe anybody does."

"No, I suppose not, although I don't think the kids notice one way or the other."

"A blessed time of life, isn't it? Few serious cares, nothing but fun and frolic, especially in summer."

"Not like being an adult," Pamela said, nodding her agreement. "We get to take care of the serious stuff so they don't have to. Do you have children?"

"No," Demetrius answered.

"Too bad," Pamela said. "I bet you'd be a good dad."

"Very kind of you to think so. That's not in the cards for me right now, but I do remember my days here as a youngster with great fondness. Being back here has renewed my appreciation for the joys of summer as a kid."

Pamela smiled. "The most romantic encounter I ever had was when I was a summer camp counselor. So intense and so thrilling. Now that I think of it, everything in our teens was intense and thrilling—such high drama."

"Largely without consequence, too," Demetrius added. "Plenty of intensity once we grow up, but now, things seem much more important."

201

"Like murder?"

"Like murder. Or like being a leader in a lovely village."

"Do you know, is Billy any closer to solving Ike Karas's murder?"

"I can't speak to that, I'm afraid. Art Shultz has made it abundantly clear that nobody can talk to anybody about an open case."

"I understand, but it's frustrating. The town's still buzzing, and I'm getting calls from folks who are convinced there's a deranged madman out there waiting to get them."

"I wish I could help," Demetrius said, "but since you brought it up, I do have a question."

"Yes?"

"Have you by chance heard anything from Mark Wells about the case?"

"No, why?"

"Just curious," Demetrius said. "We had a chat recently, and he was encouraged to make sure people are fully cooperating with Billy's investigation. I thought he might have spoken with you and your colleagues on the Council."

"No," Pamela said. "Haven't heard from him in several days."

"Huh."

"So, what you're telling me is that the case is still wide open. No progress at all?"

"Oh, I didn't say that. Progress is being made, but it is still an open case."

"Progress? Well, that's something."

Demetrius gave Pamela a wink. "It's better than none, that's for sure," he said.

Pamela's response to the wink was fleeting, but Demetrius was sure he saw distress in her eyes. He wondered if it was triggered by the prospect of progress or the fact that Mark Wells appeared to be discouraging, if not impeding, the investigation. Pamela turned and walked back to her kids and their pals; half of them were in the water before she got to her blanket. The kids all laughed and hollered; Pamela just stared absently at the water.

Chapter 20

DEMETRIUS CLIMBED INTO Billy's car. "Any chance there's a good Mexican restaurant around here?" he asked.

"Don't know. Never thought about it."

"Really? You get through your days without a good fajita, crispy tacos, maybe a Margarita? How is that possible?"

"Clean living? I don't know; stuff just isn't on my radar, I guess. High school, college, all we ate was pizza and burgers."

"But never salsa and chips? My friend, you've led a deprived life."

"If you say so."

"I do. Gimme a second." Demetrius worked his phone. "Three, four of them, right over in Vernon. Let's try the top-rated one. They have beer and wine, so we can't go wrong on that score."

"Tell me where to go."

Demetrius gave Billy the address, and they drove to a mall. After they ordered beers, Billy asked, "What should I order?"

Demetrius flipped open his menu and scanned it. "Try number six, the combination plate. You'll get chips, salsa and guac, a taco and an enchilada, and rice and beans, of course. You prefer chicken or beef?"

"Damned if I know. What's guac'?"

"Guacamole? You don't know— Wow, you weren't kidding about this, were you?"

"No. Why?"

"I don't believe I've ever known anyone who hasn't had a taco. It's amazing."

Billy blushed. And their waitress appeared.

"I'll have the number four: one chicken taco, one beef taco, rice, and beans," Demetrius said. "My bewildered friend here will have the number six, but please add an extra taco. So, that's one chicken, one beef, like mine."

"Got it," the waitress confirmed.

"And a favor, if you don't mind."

"Yeah? What?"

"Has anybody in here ordered a fajita?"

The waitress gave Demetrius a quizzical look, then answered. "The single in booth four, the guy in the painter's outfit." She pointed. "He's havin' the steak fajita. Same thing he always orders."

"Perfect," Demetrius said. "When it's ready, could you swing by our table and show it to my friend here?"

"Huh?"

"I want him to see what it looks like, what it sounds like."

"Huh?" the waitress said again.

Demetrius smiled. "My friend here has never eaten Mexican."

"Shut your mouth!"

"No kidding. Really. We're starting him off with the basics, but if you could show him a fajita . . . You serve it sizzling, right?"

"Of course."

"I'd like him to see that. For next time."

"Okay," the waitress agreed. She gave Billy a full once-over. "Never?"

"Not until this minute," Billy said. He shrugged. "What can I tell you?"

"That's just weird, man," the waitress said. She walked away, looking back at Billy twice.

"I feel like an idiot," Billy said.

"Oh, don't," Demetrius reassured him. "It's just kind of unusual, is all. No problem."

While the men waited, Billy pulled out his notes and offered a more comprehensive report on his session with Lucinda. Demetrius listened intently and asked no questions. "Why did you have me ask her this," Billy inquired.

"One of the things that's been bothering me is Karas's phone. It should have been in the house, maybe in his car, but it should have been with him. It wasn't."

"I know that."

"And we both left it at that. We missed the obvious."

"Which is?"

"Which is, if it wasn't with him, somebody must have taken it," Demetrius pointed out. "Plus, somebody told us about it, but we missed it. That's why we needed Lucinda."

"Are you telling me *she* has Karas's phone?"

"Almost certainly."

"And we know where she got it."

"We already knew. Now it's confirmed. That's why you had to talk to her."

"Okay. I mean, it's information we didn't have or that we missed, but where does—"

"It lead? It leads to Dr. Kraskin."

Billy furrowed his brow. "I don't get it."

"That's because you don't know what I learned when I spoke to him."

"You gonna tell me?"

"Of course, I am. But there's a catch."

"What?"

"It stays between us. You can't tell anybody else."

"Not even Shultz?"

"We'll get to that. But for now, it's you and me, Billy. Nobody else. Not a soul. Got it?"

"No. I mean, yes, I get it. But no, I don't understand."

The waitress appeared, carrying a steaming, sizzling iron skillet on a wooden plank. It crackled and popped and spat little droplets of oil. She stretched her arm and held it under Billy's nose. "Steak fajita," she said. "We do chicken, too, but when people ask me what I recommend, this is it. Your order's up; I'll be right back."

Billy looked at the platter and nodded. "That looks great," he said. The waitress trotted away. "How come you didn't order *that* for me?" Billy asked.

"One step at a time, my friend."

The waitress served the men's orders. Demetrius let his sit and pointed to one of the two tacos on Billy's plate. "That one first," he said. "If they're good at what they do, the chicken should be tender and spicy but definitely not dry."

Billy took a bite, scattering crumbs from the taco shell onto the table and his lap. He chewed, his eyes closed, and broke into a broad smile. "This stuff is good. Lettuce, tomato, sauce with a neat kick to it. Chicken's done just right. It's like a hot sandwich."

"Even better than that," Demetrius said. "Welcome to the world."

Billy devoured the first taco and then dipped his fork into the rice and beans, nibbled, and smiled again. "I'm lovin' that melted cheese. So, tell me about Kraskin."

Demetrius took a long pull on his Tecate and folded his

hands. "I wasn't kidding about your comment. When you said the case was making you sick, I didn't take it literally—you're as healthy as you can be—but the concept of illness stayed with me. And then, I remembered something I saw. Well, a couple of things. And it all began to make sense to me."

"All what?" Billy prodded.

"Just wait. Once you hear what Kraskin told me, you'll figure it out too."

Billy sliced his enchilada and took a bite. "Damn, that's good too. I'm comin' back here soon."

Demetrius smiled. "Good. So, here's what Kraskin told me."

While Billy ate, Demetrius explained what he had asked Kraskin to do and why. Kraskin had agreed, reluctantly, to provide the information Demetrius wanted after the doctor secured a solemn promise of confidentially that the information would be confined to Clarke and Williamson exclusively. When Demetrius finished, Billy sat back and polished off the rest of his beer. He signaled their waitress, holding up his empty and two fingers, and waited, absorbing what he'd heard until the beers arrived. "I don't believe it," he finally said.

"I know," Demetrius concurred. "It's shocking."

"You're sure? There's no way around this?"

"None that I can see. But if you see an alternative explanation, say so."

Billy paused, thought, and said, "No, it makes sense. I've got a bunch of questions, but I can't argue with it." He paused again, frowning.

Demetrius nodded. "Unsettling, isn't it?"

"It sure as hell is. I guess there's only one thing we can do now."

"Yes."

"I can't say I'm looking forward to it."

"Neither am I, Billy."

"Still—"

"Still, it has to be done."

"Brutal," Billy said. "Just brutal."

"Yes, it is.'

"First thing tomorrow, you think?"

"We don't have any choice. Yes, tomorrow morning."

"Damn."

The men finished their meal, and the waitress came back with the bill in one hand and a small plate in the other.

"What's that?" Billy asked.

"It's a flan," the waitress answered. "A kind of a custard thing—dessert, sweet and creamy. Your first time here, it's on the house."

Billy took a bite. "I like it."

"Course you do," the waitress said.

"You want a taste, Demetrius?"

Demetrius smiled. "No, thanks. It's all yours."

"Great." Billy looked at the waitress. "You guys deliver?"

The waitress smiled. "Nope. But you can call ahead, and we'll fix a carryout for you."

"Great."

"We're open for breakfast, too," the waitress added.

"Really?"

"Best chorizo scramble this side of Sonora."

"Chorizo?"

"Sausage," Demetrius said. "Start your day off with a bang."

"No kidding?" Billy took the bill from the waitress. "I'll be back, ma'am. You can count on that."

"Fine by me," the waitress said. "Don't get a lot of men

209

lookin' as good as you do 'round here. I'm Carmela. You come back, you be sure to ask for my table, okay?"

"Roger that."

As Billy pulled out of the parking lot, he slowed to a crawl. "We'll need a plan," he said. "A strategy. I don't want to get this wrong."

"Yes, of course," Demetrius agreed. "Here's how I think it should go . . ."

* * *

After a light breakfast, Demetrius left the Inn and crossed the street, turning to walk slowly down the sidewalk past the houses on the Green. He paused to admire the trees in the median and watched as the cruiser drove down the street and made a U-turn at the old Town Hall. It pulled to a stop, but Billy didn't get out.

When Demetrius came to the sidewalk leading to Tenny Baker's front porch, Billy climbed out of his cruiser, adjusted his belt, and donned his hat. His uniform's slacks and jacket were crisply creased, the badge on his chest was polished, and his white shirt was fresh and sharp. The two men walked up the sidewalk, and Demetrius knocked on the door.

Tenny Baker pulled the door open just enough to see who was knocking, smiled, and pulled it wide open. "How nice of you boys to drop by," she said. "The waffle iron is still warm. Come on in."

Billy removed his hat and laid it on a chair near the door. Tenny led them down the hall to the kitchen. Behind her, Demetrius pointed at Tenny. Billy watched her walk down the hall and nodded.

"Lovely summer day, isn't it?" Tenny said. "Look at the sun on my backyard; it makes the grass almost shine, and I

210

love the shade the apple trees throw. I may sit out there this afternoon, it's so nice."

Demetrius and Billy sat at the kitchen table while Tenny poured batter and closed the waffle iron. "Coffee for you two?" she offered. "I believe I have some orange juice in the ice box if you'd prefer that. Got a collection of tea bags, too—the bridge club drinks it."

"Coffee will be fine for me," Demetrius answered.

"Me, too," Billy said.

"Good." Tenny poured two mugs and passed them over before she went to the refrigerator and extracted a butter dish. She walked around the counter and put the dish on the table. "Syrup's in that little gravy boat, the one with the spout. I know most folks keep their syrup in the ice box, but I think it should be room temp or even warmed. Doesn't make any sense to serve a hot waffle and then pour cold liquid on it, does it?"

Neither of the men responded. Billy carefully examined the steam floating from his mug. Demetrius was gazing out the window at the apple trees in the corner of the yard.

"These four are done," Tenny announced. She sliced the square in half and then in quarters and used tongs to lay waffles on each man's plate. "I've had my breakfast already," she said. "Lately, I'm waking up earlier and earlier. Don't know why that is. You boys dig right in."

Tenny's guests each cut off a small triangle and ate it. "Delicious," Demetrius said.

"Sure is," Billy agreed. "Scrumptious."

"I'm so glad to see you both," Tenny said. "Don't get a lot of visitors these days, 'cept when Lucinda comes to do for me and when my bridge club meets, though we don't play as much in the summer. Used to have company in this house all the time: dinner parties, canasta, charades, groups meeting about this and that. Not so much these days."

Demetrius finished one waffle and laid his fork aside. "I'm not sure we qualify as company," he said.

"Oh?"

"Well, to be accurate, I guess *I'm* company. But Billy's working."

Tenny leaned back against the counter. "On what?" she inquired. "Did one of the swap meet people complain again? I keep telling them not to tramp around on my front yard, but they ignore me, and I admit that sometimes, I get kind of ornery with them. I don't mean anything by it, you know. It's just my way."

"It's not about the swap meet, ma'am," Billy said.

"No? What then? Would you like more coffee?"

"No, thank you," Billy replied. He paused, his demeanor anxious and ill-at-ease. "I want you to know I'm not happy about this, Mrs. Baker. Fact is, I'm here to interrogate you about the murder of Ike Karas."

Tenny's hands flew to her face. She covered herself from forehead to chin as if hiding. When she lowered her hands, she was pale. "Whatever about?"

"Several things, ma'am. Muffins, Mr. Karas's cell phone, and . . ." Billy paused and swallowed hard. "Cyanide."

Tenny's head, shoulders, and arms drooped, and her knees weakened a bit. Demetrius thought she might collapse, but before he could move to her, she snapped to attention and glared at Billy. "What do I know about these things? Nothing, that's what. I'm quite insulted by your attitude, young man. *Quite* insulted. You are behaving rudely."

Billy's face colored a little. His notepad lay beside his plate, and he picked it up to glance at it. "Mrs. Baker, can you please tell me where you were two weeks ago Monday between

5 and 6 in the morning?"

"Right where I always am at that hour of the morning, of course. I was in my bed. I might have been in here, in the kitchen, but I was certainly here at home. What a question."

"Yes, ma'am. Are you sure? Are you sure you didn't walk across the street to deliver a batch of blueberry muffins to Mr. Karas?"

"Of course not. I despised that fellow. Why would I share my baked goods with him?"

"Perhaps to kill him."

"Are you daft, young man?"

"No, ma'am. And neither is my friend, Mr. Clarke."

Tenny shifted her gaze to Demetrius. "*You're* in on this? I'm shocked. You're good Tolland people; you know better than to show so little respect for your elders. I don't believe it."

"I'm afraid it's true, Mrs. Baker," Demetrius replied. "I think Officer Williamson's questions are entirely appropriate. Neither of us is happy about this, but that doesn't mean we can ignore what we know."

Tenny moved around the counter to a chair at the table. She grimaced as she did so, but her pain didn't stop her as she sat, ramrod straight. She extended one arm and pointed to Demetrius first and then to Billy. "This is nonsense. I'll ask both of you to leave now. Right away. Accusing me of murder? I've never in my born days heard the likes of this. Get out."

"We can't leave yet," Billy said. "Mrs. Baker, there is evidence. You need to listen to us. Do you have a lawyer?"

"Of course, I do," Tenny said. "That fine young man down on Cider Mill Road, William Grantham, handles my affairs."

"Would you like him to be here?" Billy's question was gentle. "May I give him a call?"

"Certainly not," Tenny replied. "I have no need of his services over this . . . this . . . *outrageous* accusation. Why on earth would I need an attorney?"

"For protection," Demetrius answered. "And to make sure you understand that you don't have to talk with Billy at all if you don't want to."

"I don't care about that. There is nothing to talk about. You are both upsetting me. I want you to go now."

"We can't," Demetrius said.

"Why not?"

"Because there's ample evidence for Billy to arrest you, ma'am."

"For what?"

Billy sighed and lowered his head. He talked to the table to avoid looking Tenny in the eye. "For murder," he said.

Chapter 21

"THIS IS UTTERLY preposterous," Tenny said. The color in her cheeks rose until she was truly blushing, but there was no embarrassment in her tone. "I have never been so insulted in my life."

"Again, ma'am, we're sorry," Billy said. "But . . . we *know*. We know it all."

Tenny stared at Billy for a long moment. Then, she giggled. "Oh, I get it. This is a joke, isn't it? You two dreamed this up. I must say, you had me going for a minute there, but really, you must stop now." Billy started to speak, but Tenny shushed him and continued. "You honestly believe that a decrepit old lady who can't get around without a walker went across the street and poisoned that awful man? And then came back home and sat down to breakfast? It's just, I don't know . . . It's just silly."

Billy glanced at Demetrius, who nodded to him. Billy kept going. "Well, for one thing, it's clear that you *don't* need the walker to get around. You led us back here and moved around the kitchen for at least fifteen minutes without using your walker at all."

Tenny crooked her head to one side, then tightened her lips and firmly shook her head in disagreement. She started to speak, but Billy leaned forward and continued. "When Mr. Clarke first came to visit you, he noticed the same thing. You walked all around the house without your walker. Then, we saw you again a couple of days later. We were on the sidewalk, and you were on the porch. The walker wasn't there. It may be more comfortable for you to use it, but there's no doubt you can get around without it."

Demetrius added, "I'm sure it's more comfortable to use it, but I think there's another reason. I think you take considerable pride in walking the Green with that elegant walker. It's distinctive, it's handsome, and it forces you to stand up straight, so you look rather regal."

Tenny smiled. "I do enjoy that. But walking all the way over to that man's house and back without my wooden throne, I'm not capable of that."

Billy folded his hands and looked directly at Tenny. "Then how did you come into possession of his cell phone?" he asked.

Tenny flinched visibly. "I never—"

"Sure you did. You went to Ike's house, you met him on the back patio, and you gave him a poisoned muffin. And when he took a couple of bites of it and began to get sick, you took his phone so he couldn't call anyone for help."

"No," Tenny insisted. "No."

"Lucinda says you gave her a cell phone two days after Mr. Karas was killed. You told her that your nephew, lives in Maine, gave it to you when he got a new one but that you don't like cell phones so you weren't going to use it."

"That's true," Tenny acknowledged. "I *did* give a phone to Lucinda. But the other part, that's just nonsense. Why would I poison half a dozen muffins? Where would I even get this poison—cyanide, you say?"

"Well, we didn't tell you it was cyanide. But yes, it was cyanide," Billy said. "And I'm curious, ma'am. How do you know there were half a dozen muffins?"

Tenny's eyes darted around the room for a moment. "Somebody told me about it."

"Who?"

"I don't recall."

"I'm sorry, ma'am, but that just isn't possible. The only ones who know what we found when we searched Karas's house after he was murdered are Mr. Clarke, my boss Art Shultz, and me."

"And there's something else," Demetrius said. "There was only one muffin on the patio when the police arrived. It was the poisoned one Karas never finished. The other five had been moved into the nook in his kitchen. He died without leaving the patio. So, how did the muffins get into the house?"

"I don't have any idea," Tenny said.

"You took them in," Billy supplied. He smiled gently. "You just couldn't let them sit in the sun and go bad, could you?"

Tenny shook her head emphatically. "This is all just . . . I haven't done anything wrong. You're being absurd, both of you. Where would I get cyanide in the first place? It's just ridiculous."

Billy looked at Demetrius and raised his eyebrows. Demetrius leaned forward and spoke. "We were so certain that the cyanide was either weed killer or rat poison that we didn't do a proper investigation. At one point, we wondered if the muffins were homemade or store-bought. Finding the source of the muffins would have been helpful, but the state troopers' lab wouldn't help. Still, it got us to thinking about sources: the source of the muffins and the source of the poison. I did some research and learned something that changed our view of the case." Demetrius met Tenny's eyes and said, "You *made* the cyanide . . . right here in this kitchen."

Tenny's face went pale, and a tremor passed through her. As she struggled for control, Demetrius continued. "*Apples*, Mrs. Baker. There is cyanide in apple seeds. It takes a lot of them to create a lethal dose, but"—he smiled at her—"you've got plenty of apples." Demetrius turned in his chair and pointed to the shelf where the three bowls were filled with apples, then pivoted and pointed to the stand of apple trees in the corner of Tenny's yard. "You used a mortar and pestle to crush the seeds. Eventually, the seeds leak out a tiny amount of cyanide. It probably takes a dozen or so apples before you get enough to be harmful and even more to be lethal, but you managed that. Then, you loaded one of the muffins with the oil."

Billy spoke. "That's one reason we're certain you were there, ma'am. Ike had his choice of six muffins, but he got the poisoned one right away. You made sure of that, didn't you? You handed him the one you wanted him to eat."

Tenny's shoulders sank, and she folded down into her seat. She gasped.

Demetrius leaned over and picked up Tenny's coffee cup. "Take a sip," he said.

Tenny did. And when she had caught her breath, Billy asked her again, "You did make sure he ate the right muffin, didn't you?"

Tenny jutted her chin out and barely nodded. Both men waited. "Yes," she answered. "Karas was an awful man who had no business living in this village, never mind on the Green. He was crude and ill-mannered, and what he did to that beautiful house . . ." Tenny's breathing was ragged, and her anger was fierce. She composed herself slowly. "I could see it all from my porch, you know. Dozens of workmen tearing the place apart, knocking down walls until, one day, I could look in his front window and see all the way to the patio. It was a crime, what he did. No respect for values or tradition or decency."

"Ike Karas wasn't Tolland people," Demetrius concurred.
"Certainly not!"

"But that doesn't excuse what you've done," Billy said.
"Even in Tolland, a crime is a crime."

Tenny regarded Billy intently. "See? That's what I mean,"
she said. "You're good for Tolland. You keep us safe, and you
make sure we behave properly, and you're fair and sensible
and honest. That terrible man was none of those things." The
fire went out of her eyes. "But you're right. I was protecting
Tolland."

The three sat in silence for several minutes. Tenny's eyes
teared up, but she was determined to maintain control. She
didn't quite cry.

After a pause, Billy nodded to Demetrius, who broke the
silence. "Mrs. Baker, may I ask you a personal question?"

Tenny smiled weakly. "As if this isn't personal enough,
Rusty? What now?"

"I'm concerned about your health, ma'am. I have a sense
that you're not well, and while Billy has to do his job, I'm
worried that the stress and strain will—"

"Kill me?"

"I wasn't going to say that. I'm worried that the stress will
make your condition worse."

"What condition? What are you talking about?"

Billy looked anxious. Demetrius saw it and held up his
hand before Billy intervened.

"Mrs. Baker, I'm a writer. One of the benefits—or maybe
it's a curse—is that I can't stop observing people. I see quirks, I
see odd behavior, I see normal people doing normal things, and
I see abnormal, too. A few days ago, I walked past your porch
while you were napping. I watched you, and I couldn't ignore

what I saw. I saw someone who isn't well, isn't well at all."

This time, Tenny did cry. Slowly, tears leaked down her cheeks, and she extracted a handkerchief from a sleeve and dabbed. "I remember you being a bright young thing," she said, "and I was right. And . . . so are you."

"Tell me about it," Demetrius urged.

And Tenny did.

* * *

Standing on the porch after they had pulled the front door shut, Billy turned to Demetrius and said, "'Observing people,' eh? Pretty slick."

Demetrius smiled. "I made a promise to Dr. Kraskin, and I was not going to break it. I thought if I just asked her, she might confirm what he told me. She did."

"Yes."

"So, now it's out in the open, and Kraskin is off the hook."

"As I say, pretty slick."

"Maybe. But it wasn't anything compared to what comes next. And you'll be on your own in the 'slick' department at the next gathering."

Billy checked his watch. "Shultz won't be at his desk for another hour," he said. "Let's scoot down the street and get a pizza."

"Fortification before you do battle?"

"Something like that."

"Well, why not?"

The men went down the steps toward the cruiser. Demetrius stopped at the end of Tenny's sidewalk and turned back. As he watched, the curtains in the living room slowly moved together until there was nothing to see but masked windows. A moment later, the same thing happened in the dining room.

Chapter 22

"**Y**OU'RE KIDDING ME," Art Shultz said. "*That* old bat? The one with that Rolls Royce walker? No way."

"She's confirmed it, sir," Billy informed his boss. "We would have made the case without that, but there's no doubt at all now. She confessed."

"I'll be damned. You got any idea why?"

"Standards. Ike Karas did not measure up to her standards for Tolland."

"That's a motive?"

"In this case, there is no doubt. She's lived here all her life. I believe she's third-generation Tolland. The town means everything to her. She couldn't live with what Karas represented, the way he treated the townspeople, the ugly changes to his house. It was too much for her."

Shultz snorted.

Billy gave Shultz a full briefing—Tenny's ability to move without the walker, the cell phone and her knowledge of the precise number of muffins (which both proved she'd been in Karas's house), and the little apple grove in her yard that yielded the cyanide. "I've got the lab checking the muffin," Billy said. "They think they can get back to me today, and no doubt they'll confirm that the cyanide that killed Karas came from apples. Rex—he's the guy I deal with there—thinks they may even be able to tie the poison directly to the type of apples she grows."

"Unbelievable," Schultz replied. "So, she's under arrest, right? She got a lawyer yet?"

Billy shifted in his chair before he spoke. "Um . . . no. She's at home."

"*What?* A confessed murderer, and you let her walk? Pick her up, Williamson. Now!"

"I'd prefer not to do that," Billy said.

"I don't give a damn what you'd prefer, kid. Get her in custody while I talk to our communications people and the DA's office. We'll announce the arrest first thing tomorrow."

"I don't think that's advisable, sir," Billy asserted.

Shultz looked as if he might levitate and attack. He glared at Billy. Billy remained calm and waited, though his stomach was churning. "Why not?" Schultz asked. "And just who the hell do you think you—"

Billy sat up in his chair. "She's dying, sir. She'll never go to trial."

"The hell you say?"

Billy turned to Demetrius and said, "*You* tell him."

"Commander," Demetrius began, "once we had most of the pieces in place—apple seeds making cyanide, a plausible motive, the cell phone she swiped—I still wasn't convinced. I was as surprised as you are. I couldn't shake the idea that it just didn't make sense."

"What's the issue? You got the weapon, and you got her on Karas's patio the day he died. According to Williamson, there's a strong motive, too. And a confession. What's wrong, Clarke?"

"Think about it. Mrs. Baker is the primmest, most proper lady in this village, and she relishes her status here. She's the grand dame, the font of native wisdom, and the town's true champion. And she is so proud of her place in the community. I think the current phrase is 'street cred,' and she's got it in abundance."

"So what? What's your point?"

"A week or so ago, I saw her on her porch. She was dozing, and she looked terrible: pale and drawn. She just wasn't the same person I knew. Then, a few days later, I saw Doctor Kraskin. He'd just come out of her house, and he was carrying his doc bag with him, so it seemed logical that he was there professionally. Before he got in his car, everything about him said he was agonized. He was so sad that it weighed him down. I cannot— No, I *will* not tell you what happened next. But it isn't important any longer."

"You're not making sense, Clarke."

"Sorry. What I *can* tell you is that Hortense Baker has told us that she is ravaged with cancer, that it has engulfed her completely. It's why Kraskin was treating her, and he knew there was no hope. There is nothing to be done for her except make her last days as comfortable as possible. Since she has freely shared that information with us, you are free to confirm it with Dr. Kraskin if you wish."

Shultz, fully attentive, nodded and grunted once.

"The point is, sir," Demetrius continued, "that Mrs. Baker was prepared to eliminate what she believed was a scourge on her beloved community because she had nothing to lose. She's already under a death sentence. If she weren't dying, I don't think she'd have done what she did."

"So, we just let it slide? I'm not about to have an unsolved murder on my watch until I retire. We have a duty to perform. Right, Officer Williamson?"

"Yes sir, we do," Billy agreed. "The question is, how best to perform it."

"And you're going to tell me, are you?"

"I do have a suggestion, sir. If Mrs. Baker goes anywhere, she'll move to a hospice. But I don't think she's ever going to leave her house again. Mr. Clarke agrees. So, we have a choice. We could arrest her."

"Yes, that's our job."

"It is, sir, but think about it. You know how this town works. If we arrest her, the whole village will know about it in no time at all, and then we'll be the hard-hearted goons who put a respected woman in a cell to die rather than letting her die in peace at home. We'll also be the guys who destroyed the one thing she values more than any other: her good name. At best, that'll look pretty damn mean. I'm not saying we should ignore what she did, but I think it would be cruel in the extreme to arrest her right now. Can you imagine what your friend Ginny Irving would do with that? I can. It's not pretty."

Art Shultz leaned back in his chair. He swiveled it back and forth several times before he spoke. "So, what's your recommendation?" he finally asked.

"House arrest. We secure her promise that she will not leave the house. We could even put an ankle bracelet on her, if you insist. Then, you invite Ms. Irving to an interview, and you tell her that the department has identified the killer and an arrest is imminent, pending the final stages of investigation. You assure the good people of Tolland that you have the suspect under constant surveillance, so the village and its residents are safe. And you promise Ms. Irving that as soon as an arrest is made, she will be given the complete story."

"And then we wait?"

Billy nodded. "We wait."

Shultz turned to Demetrius. "You come up with this, Clarke?"

Demetrius shook his head. "No, sir. I admire its compassion, and I think it is the most respectful way to deal with an extremely difficult situation, but the plan is Officer Williamson's. He's dedicated to protecting Tolland, and he's smart enough to know that it takes goodwill and common sense to do that as well as he possibly can. We can check with Kraskin, but I don't think it will be more than a week or so before you can announce that the case is solved and that the killer is no longer a threat. When you make that announcement, you can tell everyone that you elected to let her die at home out of respect for her years of dedicated service and contributions to her community. It's neat, it's clean, and it's best for everyone involved. Including you."

Shultz sat back and swiveled some more. He picked up a pen and twirled it through his fingers, then stared at the ceiling. Then, he set the pen aside and picked up a paper clip, twisting it until it was one long sliver of metal. His silence filled the room.

"If I may, sir," Demetrius said, "I believe the phrase you're searching for is 'Good job, Officer.'"

Shultz scowled at Demetrius. Then, he stood and leaned across his desk, his hand extended. "Good work, Williamson. We'll do it your way. If it goes wrong, I'm going to lay it at your feet. But I don't think it will. Truth is, you've done good work here, your first major crime at that. And letting Tenny sit at home is unorthodox, but it's also pretty smart." Shultz frowned as something crossed his mind. "Almost forgot, Williamson. When we're done here, you need to stop by Detective Wolinsky's desk."

"Why?"

"Tell him I said he's not being transferred to the Karas murder case. Tell him it's been solved."

Billy grinned.

Shultz turned to face Demetrius. "And you, Clarke. I got a question for you."

"Shoot."

"You leaving town soon?"

Demetrius laughed. "I've extended my stay here well beyond my original plan. So, yes, I'll be headed home as soon as I can make arrangements."

"Good. Get out of here, both of you. I have work to do."

* * *

Hortense Baker died before Virginia Irving finished writing up her interview with Art Shultz. Ginny's complete story about the murder of Ike Karas appeared the day before a memorial service for Tenny. Most of Tolland attended the service in the church on the Green. The casket was closed, and Tenny's walker stood next to it, polished and glowing.

After the service concluded, Will Grantham worked through the gathering on the lawn in front of the church until he found Demetrius, Billy Williamson, and Art Shultz standing quietly off to one side. "Mr. Clarke? I'm Will Grantham, and I'm the executor of Mrs. Baker's will. May I have a word with you?"

"Sure," Demetrius said while shaking the lawyer's hand.

"In private," Grantham insisted.

Demetrius smiled. "There's no need for that. I trust these two gentlemen, so say what you will. If they misuse what they hear, we both know where to find them, right?"

Grantham smiled. "Fine. I am instructed to sell Mrs. Baker's house on the Green. The proceeds are to be divided among three nieces and a nephew."

"Why are you telling me this?"

"Because there's a specific reference to you in those instructions, sir. I am instructed to tell you that you are granted first right of refusal on the property. Further, if you exercise your option to purchase, I am instructed to have the property appraised by Mrs. Bondurant and to reduce her appraised sale price by 25 percent."

Demetrius's mouth fell open.

Billy Williamson let out a whoop and punched Demetrius on the shoulder. "Man, that's great," he exclaimed. "Jump on it, Clarke. Jump on it."

Art Shultz said, "He's going to *live* here? Just what I need." He threw up his arms in feigned disgust.

Grantham said, "There's one more item. A binding codicil."

"What's that?" Demetrius asked.

"If and when you purchase the house, you are obligated to—and these are her words—you are 'obligated to nurture, preserve, and protect the stand of apple trees in the backyard.'"

"You're kidding."

"No, sir. I agree that it's quite unusual. Indeed, I was so curious that I asked her to explain it."

"What did she say?"

"She said to tell you, and I'm directly quoting her again: 'You never know.'"

The lawyer grinned, and Demetrius, Billy, and Shultz broke into loud laughter.

"I'm quite overwhelmed," Demetrius said. "I certainly didn't anticipate this. Plus, I'm flying back to LA tomorrow. Do you need my answer now?"

"No, sir. There are some other bequests—charities and such—that need to be executed. I imagine I'll need at least a week, perhaps two, before I'm done. I've been in touch with the nieces and nephew, and they understand what Mrs. Baker wanted. They are content to wait while you decide what to do."

"That's generous," Demetrius said. "I'll need to think this over since it's such a big step. Give me some time to consider it. Can I get back to you in, say, ten days?"

"Perfect."

Grantham shook hands with Demetrius again and then moved back toward the gathering.

"I'll be damned," Demetrius said.

"Nah," Billy said, "you won't be damned. You'll be Tolland people for real. What do you say we motor on over to that Mexican place? I'm starving."

"A fine idea," Demetrius agreed. "Let's go."

* * *

Katherine Conrad ran Demetrius's credit card through her system while Demetrius wandered over to the buffet in the living room and poured himself a small cup of coffee. "All done," Katherine announced. "It's been a pleasure having you stay with us, Mr. Clarke, and I do hope you'll visit us again soon."

Jeff Conrad came out of the kitchen. His overalls were the same, but he had put on a fresh tee shirt; instead of red, it was maroon. "Don't cha'ge him for the extra days."

"I didn't, dear. Just the four nights he booked, no more."

"Good on ya." Jeff reached into the pocket of his overalls and extracted a business card. He walked up to Demetrius and extended one hand for a shake, the card in the other. The men shook hands, and Demetrius looked at the card. It was Jeff Conrad's woodworking business card. "Turn it ovah," Jeff said.

Demetrius did.

"Says first two nights are free, your next visit he-ah. It's a gift cod."

From the Publisher

Thank You from the Publisher

Van Rye Publishing, LLC ("VRP") sincerely thanks you for your interest in and purchase of this book.

VRP hopes you will please consider taking a moment to help other readers like you by leaving a rating or review of this book at your favorite online book retailer. You can do so by visiting the book's product page and locating the button for leaving a rating or review.

Thank you!

Resources from the Publisher

Van Rye Publishing, LLC ("VRP") offers the following resources to readers and to writers.

For *readers* who enjoyed this book or found it useful, please consider receiving updates from VRP about new and discounted books like this one. You can do so by following VRP on Facebook (at www.facebook.com/vanryepub), Twitter (at www.twitter.com/vanryepub), or Instagram (at www.instagram.com/vanryepub).

For *writers* who enjoyed this book or found it useful, please consider having VRP edit, format, or fully publish your book manuscript. You can find out more and submit your manuscript at VRP's website (at www.vanryepublishing.com).

Thank you again!

About the Author

D AVID M. HAMLIN is the author of three *Emily Winter* mysteries: *Winter in Chicago*, *Winter Gets Hot*, and *Killer Cocktail*. He has also written a wide range of freelance news and feature articles for daily and weekly newspapers. David's work in short stories and flash fiction has been published in several literary journals. Earlier in his writing career, he also wrote two nonfiction books, *The Nazi/Skokie Conflict* and *Los Angeles's Original Farmers Market*, and a political satire column.

Prior to his work in fiction, David fashioned a career in activism. In the 1960s, he served in VISTA (the domestic peace corps). He spent nearly a decade as an Executive Director of the American Civil Liberties Union (ACLU) in New Hampshire and Illinois. He was then a partner in a Los Angeles public relations agency that specialized in non-profit advocacy and social change campaigns. David has also stocked shelves in a grocery store, sold small appliances, been a Kelly Girl, been part of a work crew raising power poles in rural Maine, and worked in a pizza parlor (he can still toss a crust in the air without tearing it).

David lives, writes, plays tennis, and devours crossword puzzles in Palm Springs, CA. He is married to Sydney Weisman, a former journalist, award-winning publicist, and delightful cabaret performer. He can be reached via www.dmhwrites.com.